The Cataphract Oath

I0570721

Marc Edmond Best

To all the friends and family who have kept pushing me forward on this new adventure.

CHAPTER ONE

"What a lovely day for a war."

Professor Dorrett's bright smile parted his wind-ruffled beard. He wasn't the only one in a good mood; the entirety of Osterbridge's citizenry had dressed in their best silken finery and crowded onto the city walls to watch the impending battle.

"If you say so, sir." Teenager-gangly and bespectacled, Victor looked every inch the professor's assistant. He followed Professor Dorrett's gaze--not out over the eastward plains and the approaching army, but to the other spectators lined up along the battlements.

The atmosphere was more of a festival than a siege. Enterprising vendors set up charcoal braziers and cooking pots, offering various fried delicacies and mugs of spiced wine. Musicians strolled amongst the crowd, strumming out old standbys like "The Song of the Huntress' Saber" and "The Love-Struck Cuirassier." A troupe of jugglers flipped balls, knives, and clubs through the air while a lithe acrobat tumbled and flipped between the flying objects. Soldiers swaggered through the crowd in shining dress uniform, paying more attention to the well dressed ladies in the crowd than to the army massed in the distance.

The men on the walls were a mere formality. Everyone knew the Cataphracts would do the real fighting.

Just outside the city walls, the metal titans waited for the enemy. Standing over three stories tall, each was armed with an equally massive weapon: spears as long as ships' masts, or enormous swords heavy enough to cleave through houses. The Cataphracts were draped with embroidered pennants and banners that bore their unique sigils. There was the gray tower of the *Stalwart*, the coin-and-dagger of the *Guilt of Gold*, the leaping hound of the *Huntress*, and several more besides.

The Cataphracts remained statue-still, but the faint trails of smoke rising from the vents on their backs showed their alchemical furnaces were lit and ready to spur the monumental weapons into action. Half of the machines still had their visors open, allowing their pilots to bark last-minute orders to their crews, who scrambled up and down the machines, making final preparations before the battle started.

Professor Dorret snapped his long, nimble fingers at his assistant.

1

"You brought the glass, didn't you, Victor? I want to get a good look at whom the Brethren have sent to kill us."

Victor fumbled through his overstuffed leather satchel and pulled out a brass telescope the length of his forearm. He handed it over to Professor Dorrett, careful not to drop the expensive piece of equipment. The bearded academic squinted into the eyepiece, fixing his gaze on the enemy army fast approaching. He made a few pensive, wordless sounds to himself as he took the sight in, and then handed the glass back to Victor.

"Tell me what you see."

Victor raised the telescope to his right eye. In the distance, the Brethren army advanced, the column of their army crawling across the countryside like a vast, black-scaled serpent, headed straight for the city of Osterbridge. He swept his gaze over the approaching army, counting the black and yellow banners flying from hoisted lances.

"It looks like they've brought ... five or six thousand pikemen, a detachment of arquebusiers, and half again as many cavalry."

"And?" Professor Dorrett said.

Victor counted the gargantuan figures marching on either side of the infantry column. "And over a dozen Cataphracts."

"What kind?"

"Seven skirmishers, four duelists, and--" Victor focused on a pair of enormous, lumbering machines bringing up the rear of the Brethren army. Between the distance and the road dust, he couldn't make out many details--but he didn't have to. The two Cataphracts at the rear of the column easily dwarfed the others in the Brethren army (not to mention Osterbridge's own champions). Victor didn't know if it was his imagination or not, but he could feel each ponderously heavy footfall of the enormous machines. Based on the size alone, Victor knew exactly what they were.

"Siegebreakers. Two of them."

Professor Dorrett nodded. "Good eye. They've sanded her sigils off, but I'm fairly certain the one on the right is the Waiting Gallows."

"I haven't heard of her," Victor said.

"You wouldn't have. The Waiting Gallows belongs to one of the Freeholder princes--I forget which one. The Brethren must have stolen her somehow. Bastards. They must mean business if they've got that much tonnage. Just one siegebreaker's enough to level the city. Two is overkill."

"They've brought twice the tonnage that we have." Victor's mouth went dry.

"Ah, my boy. You forget something. We may be outnumbered, but the Brethren are outclassed." To prove his point, Professor Dorrett merely nodded to where the *Huntress* stood a dozen yards away.

Despite her name, there was little feminine about the *Huntress*; she was a broad-shouldered, stout-legged machine, majestic in her invincibility. Her steel armor was painted an immaculate, shining white, so polished it nearly hurt the eye to look at her too long. The *Huntress'* visor was open, offering Victor a glimpse of her lean, silver-haired captain. Unlike some of the other captains, the man at the *Huntress'* helm didn't wave or posture for the audience along the city wall; he kept his eyes on the approaching army.

Professor Dorrett went on, as if in a lecture hall. "We are currently protected by some of the best Cataphract captains to ever pick up a sword, and they're helming some of the finest machines Leovaix has to offer, which have been expertly designed and maintained by the finest minds Leovaix has to offer. Which is to say, us." He stroked his beard, considering his words. "Perhaps not you and I personally--I'm too old to muck about turning wrenches, and you're too young, but only the best are allowed to so much as touch our Cataphracts. That alone makes a world of difference."

"Of course, sir," said Victor.

"In contrast, consider the Brethren of the Chain." Professor Dorrett said. "They've got to steal their machines, since they're not smart enough to build their own. The Brethren shackle their minds just as surely as they shackle their wrists. Hell, those bastards don't even name their Cataphracts. How they expect to win a war like that, I couldn't tell you."

"I hope you're right." Victor leaned over the edge of the wall and watched the engineering crews below. As the war machines stoked their alchemical furnaces and prepared for battle, their crews scattered, retreating back through the open gates. Victor searched for a flash of golden hair among them. His friend Marissa was a few years older than he was (not to mention something of a prodigy when it came to metalwork), and as such had graduated to working on a Cataphract's crew. The question was, which one? The *Rakehell*? The *Stalwart*? Victor wished he could remember.

Someday, Victor would join her-- join them, the talented and brilliant alchemical engineers who kept the enormous war machines running and thus kept the people of Leovaix safe. Once the last of the engineering crews made it inside the city walls, the heavy gates closed, leaving only six duelist-class Cataphracts to fend off the approaching enemy.

The Brethren army fanned out from both sides of the main road, arraying themselves into formation. The infantry and cavalry gathered into large blocks, with the Cataphracts towering behind them. The ranks parted, and a dozen men carried a large palanquin through the center of the army, towards the walls of Osterbridge. Victor trained the spyglass on the palanquin--and the large, jowly man upon it. Golden chains hung from his arms, a contrast to the iron shackles that bound the palanquin bearers to their burden. A rectangular brass box was set into the man's broad chest, polished to shine almost as brightly as his gold did.

The delegation stopped just outside of musket range of the walls, close enough that Victor could hear their chains jangle. The big man pushed himself to his feet, and his golden chains rattled around him, showing how he was bound to the palanquin. In turn, a long, slack rope snaked from the back of the palanquin, winding across the dusty road, connecting the messenger to the rest of the Brethren army.

"So they've brought a Speaker? This should be good for a laugh." Professor Dorrett grinned. "Get out the wine, lad."

Victor produced a bottle and a pair of tin mugs from his pack. Somehow, he managed to pour the drinks out without his hands shaking too much. As the Brethren neared the city walls, Victor's pulse pounded faster and faster--even if Professor Dorrett and the rest of the audience didn't seem to share his anxiety.

"People of Osterbridge, rejoice!" The Speaker's voice boomed, enhanced by the metal box grafted to his chest by alchemical surgery. "Today is a glorious day--for today is your chance to change your lives, change the world for the better! For too long, you have walked in darkness, ignorant and alone! For too long, you have been led astray by the greedy and the blasphemous! For too long, your lives have been without meaning, without purpose! You are like ships that have gone adrift: sails slack, oars broken, left to the cruel mercy of the sea! But! Cry not, you fortunate souls! For I shall be your anchor, and I shall bind you with the chain of meaning!" The man raised his hands above his head, displaying the golden shackles locked around his wrists. "Join us! Join the Brethren of the Chain and link

4

yourself to your fellow man! Surrender your weapons, open your gates, and you shall be joyously connected to the whole of mankind!"

The people on the battlements replied with a salvo of creative obscenities and flung pastry. The half-eaten sweets fell well short of their target, but the invective still hit home, to judge by the way the man on the palanquin drew himself up taller, then crossed his arms over his chest.

Professor Dorrett spat over the edge of the battlements, then looked over at Victor. "Notice how he hasn't mentioned who's holding the other end of his leash. The Brethren never do. Not until they've slapped the chains on."

Below, the Speaker waited for the jeers to die down before continuing. "You prolong the inevitable! By the end of this day, each and every one of you shall be linked--or you shall die. Make the right choice now, before it is too late!"

The *Huntress* replied first.

She moved with the smooth fluidity that only came from untold hours of careful maintenance, each control cable and motive gear in perfect alignment. The *Huntress* balanced her saber on one shoulder with her right hand and raised her left up into the air. Mechanically articulated fingers curled into the drover's salute--an obscene hand sign meant to suggest a lewd (and anatomically improbable) act. The audience on the wall laughed and cheered at the hook-fingered gesture. Victor could only marvel at the amount of craftsmanship that must have gone into building and maintaining that kind of flexibility. Most Cataphracts only had enough articulation in their fingers to hold a weapon, sometimes no more than a glorified lock clamp. Victor marveled--if the *Huntress* could effortlessly hoist up the drover's salute, how would she perform in combat?

The man on the palanquin sputtered, his booming voice trailing off. He snapped his fingers at his bearers, and they scurried back to the Brethren's line as fast as they could. In turn, the Brethren's Cataphracts lurched into motion, lumbering towards the city. The *Huntress* advanced out to meet them, taking the lead as other Cataphracts fell in behind. Thunderous footsteps shook the ground as the Cataphracts marched to battle, and clouds of blue alchemical smoke puffed from the exhaust vents in their backs.

The Brethren's skirmishers, light Cataphracts barely half again the height of a man, loped ahead of the main line. They circled around the *Huntress*, jabbing their long lances at the larger Cataphract's knees and

5

ankles in an attempt to jam the comparatively delicate joints. One of the skirmishers got too close, and the *Huntress* cut it down with a single stroke. The skirmisher crumpled to the ground in two broken pieces, and a fresh cheer rose from the battlements.

First blood claimed, the *Huntress* fought on.

She built up momentum with each stride towards the enemy line, a bladed avalanche in motion. Another of the Brethren's Cataphracts--this one a duelist to match the *Huntress*' size--lunged forward with a barbed spear. Steel cleaved into oak as the *Huntress* deflected the blow with practiced ease. The *Huntress* levered the spearpoint to the side, then stepped past her opponent's guard to smash her free hand into the other duelist's visor. Metal bent beneath the *Huntress*' knuckles, and her opponent reeled back a step. The *Huntress* pressed her advantage and brought her saber around in an overhead slash. The heavy blade sank deep into the inside of the other Cataphract's elbow joint, and its hand fell slack as the *Huntress*' blade bit into control cables and motive gears. The white armored machine ripped her saber free, then struck the same point again, this time severing the arm completely.

The *Huntress*' nameless, undecorated opponent shoved away from her with its good arm, then backpedaled to make way for two of its fellows to engage. The *Huntress* met them with raised saber, and once again the clash of hardened steel echoed over the battlefield. Soon, the *Rakehell*, the *Guilt of Gold*, and the rest joined the battle, and the ensuing din only grew louder as the war machines of both sides tried to batter each other into submission. As Professor Dorrett had predicted, Osterbridge's protectors made up for their lesser numbers with sheer skill and ferocity.

The Brethren's Cataphracts fell back under the furious assault, and the Brethren infantry was forced to do the same to avoid being trampled beneath the enormous war machines. The *Rakehell* toppled one of the enemy duelists with a spear thrust to its knee joint, and the *Guilt of Gold* staved in the fallen Cataphract's cockpit with a double-handed blow from her longsword. The *Stalwart* stabbed another duelist beneath its arm while the *Huntress* accounted for two more downed skirmishers. Back on the city walls, Osterbridge's residents cheered, waving hats and scarves in the air in fresh celebration with each kill.

"What did I tell you, lad?" Professor Dorrett said. "We've got the bastards outclassed. Always have. They're falling apart even quicker than I thought."

"But what about the siegebreakers?" Victor frowned, then took the spyglass from the professor to get a better look. He squinted through the clouds of exhaust smoke, looking past the battling titans. The two towering siegebreakers still waited placidly, even as the Brethren infantry retreated past their ankles. "They haven't moved."

"Maybe they can't move." Professor Dorrett drained his mug of wine. "It's damned hard to get even a skirmisher operating correctly, much less a machine as large as a siegebreaker. I wouldn't be surprised if some idiot Brethren hadn't let their furnaces go out or got their motive gears locked up somehow."

"But their furnaces are still burning. I can see the smoke," Victor said. "It's like they're waiting for--oh."

On the other side of the battlefield, the siegebreakers began to move, venting thick clouds of exhaust as they strode across the battlefield. The Brethren's skirmishers and duelists broke off from their opponents, giving the siegebreakers room to wade in, swinging their massive rock axes. Built to smash down stone walls, the heavy weapons dealt with steel plating just as easily. The *Stalwart* lost an arm to a heavy, shearing blow, and the *Rakehell* took a hit to the center of her breastplate, hard enough to fling her backward a dozen feet. She landed in a tangle of metal limbs, then burst into searing blue flames as her alchemical furnace exploded.

A pall fell over the crowd as they watched the *Rakehell* burn. Victor swallowed and hoped the impact of the blow had killed the *Rakehell*'s captain outright, that he wasn't trapped at his machine's helm, consumed by impossibly hot alchemical flame.

One of the siegebreakers kept swinging, fending off the *Guilt of Gold* and her companions. The other split off, marching past the melee.

And towards Osterbridge.

Further down the wall, a man screamed in incoherent panic as he realized just what was happening. One siegebreaker, along with the remaining skirmishers and duelists, could easily keep the *Huntress* and company occupied long enough for the second one to march to the walls and bash them to rubble--along with anyone unfortunate enough to still be standing on them. More screams ensued, and the crowds along the battlements pushed and wrestled with each other, desperate to get to the stairs first. More than a few people were shoved off the walls entirely, plummeting the full three-story drop to crash into the food stalls below. The soldiers brave or unlucky enough to still stand on the walls shouldered their muskets and fired in the Brethren's general direction. The siegebreaker's thick armor protected it from the volley, but there was always an infinitesimally small chance a musket ball might shoot through one of the viewing gaps in the Cataphract's visor and kill her captain at the helm.

They weren't that lucky. The siegebreaker kept moving.

"We've got to get out of here!" Victor tugged at Professor Dorrett's sleeve, but the old academic didn't move.

"And go where?" Professor Dorrett said. "Even if we make it off the wall without breaking our necks, there's still a whole damn army of Brethren waiting to kill or collar us. Besides, we're not done yet. Look."

Victor followed the Professor's pointing finger. The *Huntress* still stood defiantly in front of the Brethren line. Her white armor was dented and torn, but the duelist still moved, still fought as smoothly as when the battle started. One of the siegebreakers closed in and swung its rock axe at the *Huntress*, but she sidestepped the blow, and the heavy weapon sank deep into the ground. Before the siegebreaker could pull it free, the *Huntress* reversed her grip on her saber, then stabbed the point straight through a gap in the siegebreaker's wrist joint. A quick wrench of the blade mangled the control cables within, and the siegebreaker's left hand went limp. The *Huntress* yanked her sword clear and dodged behind the bigger machine before it could react. The saber flashed again as the *Huntress* repeated the process on the back of the siegebreaker's right knee. More control cables snapped, and the *Huntress* slammed her shoulder into the siegebreaker, knocking it off balance. It tottered in the air for a long, terrible moment, then fell forward, crushing an unlucky skirmisher beneath it. The towering war machine hit the ground with a hellacious crash of steel plating and shattered gearworks. Even up on the city wall, Victor could feel the impact of the siegebreaker as it hit the ground.

Professor Dorrett clapped Victor on the shoulder and laughed. Those brave or unlucky enough to still stand on Osterbridge's walls stared at the sight, then let out a desperate, relieved cheer, their hope renewed by the sudden turn in the battle.

The *Huntress* kept moving.

She left her sword lodged in the siegebreaker's knee, instead bending down to grab its discarded rock axe. Metal strained and groaned, and a steady stream of alchemical smoke poured out of the *Huntress'* exhaust vents as her furnace pushed its limits, straining to move the heavy weapon. Even with that extra effort, the *Huntress* could only drag the rock axe, plowing a wide furrow in the ground as she marched towards the city walls.

And the second siegebreaker.

Alerted by the impact of its companion, the second siegebreaker stopped short of Osterbridge's walls, instead turning about to face the new threat--though at its size, the process was a slow one.

A Brethren skirmisher dashed across the battlefield to buy the siegebreaker time. The lighter machine harried the *Huntress*, stabbing at her with its long spear. With both hands hauling the oversized axe, the *Huntress* could do little to defend herself as the skirmisher's spear probed at her joints, occasionally slipping past armor plating to punch into the intricate machinery beneath. The *Huntress* staggered as the spearpoint broke off in her hip, but she limped on. Even slowed by the oversized weapon, the *Huntress* caught up to the other siegebreaker before it could turn completely around. The *Huntress* planted her broad feet, then braced both arms around the rock axe's haft, bringing it to bear. Even with her furnace pumping away at full blast, there was no way a Cataphract the *Huntress*' size could hope to wield the weapon with any amount of finesse.

So she didn't.

Instead, the *Huntress* thrust the head of the rock axe between the siegebreaker's legs and circled to one side, using the shaft of the polearm to trip the huge Cataphract. A smaller, nimbler machine would have been able to keep its balance. Even a siegebreaker could have managed, if it weren't for the fact that the *Huntress*' target was already in motion, turning away from the city walls. The siegebreaker stumbled forwards and fell, plowing into the ground. The earth shook, hard enough to make Victor's teeth rattle. He braced himself on the edge of the parapet and looked down at the *Huntress* and her quarry.

The *Huntress* dropped her stolen rock axe and closed in. She curled her intricately engineered fingers into a steel fist and smashed a punch into the siegebreaker's visor. She landed another blow and another still, methodically pounding at the siegebreaker's visor, until one final punch smashed through the metal canopy. Scarlet gore stained the *Huntress*' white-painted gauntlet as she raised a victorious fist to the sky. What remained of the Brethren Armor halted in their tracks, realizing they were far too late to save their larger comrade. The last few duelists and skirmishers promptly turned and ran, rather than face the *Huntress*' nigh-unstoppable wrath.

The rest of the Brethren army followed in retreat. The infantry stumbled over the chains holding them together, while the Speaker bellowed at his palanquin bearers to run faster. The *Guilt of Gold* rallied Osterbridge's remaining defenders and set about turning that retreat into a rout. Without support from their own Cataphracts, the Brethren were helpless against the towering war machines. The *Stalwart*, even short an arm, easily stomped bloody carnage through the panicked infantry, while the *Guilt of Gold* cut down whole rows of pikemen at a time with wide, scything sweeps of her sword. Osterbridge's citizenry scrambled back to the battlements in order to cheer their armored champions once again.

"What did I tell you, lad?" Professor Dorrett pushed a mug of wine into Victor's hands. "Outclassed!"

At the bottom of the wall, the *Huntress* slumped to one knee as smoke streamed from her vents, hot enough to tint the metal red. The *Huntress'* visor opened, and more smoke poured out. The *Huntress'* captain emerged, coughing and hacking, though he still had enough strength to raise his hat in salute to the city walls.

Again, the crowds cheered, and more than a few ladies leaned over the parapets to toss flowers and silk handkerchiefs in his general direction. The city gates opened, and several crewmen rushed out to lean a ladder against the *Huntress'* breastplate. The pilot managed to climb down on his own, but two young engineers supported him on either side once he got to the ground. Outside of his machine, the Cataphract captain looked impossibly small and vulnerable.

Victor felt the same way.

CHAPTER 2

SEVERAL YEARS LATER

Victor reviewed his checklist, then did the same to his workbench. Everything looked to be in order, which is what made him nervous. Given the intricate machinery he worked with, the tiniest error could set off a cascade of exponentially increasing disasters, perhaps enough to burn everything in the university workshop to cinders.

And if that happened, he wouldn't graduate.

Victor forced his fingers to remain steady as he reviewed his checklist a fourth (or was it a fifth?) time, before the faculty arrived. He made sure the miniature alchemical furnace was kindled, and more importantly, contained. While the alchemical furnace was far too small to power even a skirmisher, it had still been gifted to the university by the king himself, and was therefore invaluable.

If Victor were to damage such a gift, then he definitely wouldn't graduate.

Victor noted the readings from the pressure valves and compared them with his previous calculations to verify they were still within acceptable parameters. The tangle of piping that ran from the furnace to the motive gears showed no leaks, and the lengths of steel wire connecting the motive gears to the armature's joints were stretched to the proper tension. While the alchemical furnace was comically small, the armature was full-size; Victor had borrowed one from one of the rigs used to train would-be Cataphract captains. Long as Victor was tall, the oak and iron arm was mounted firmly to a wooden scaffold. The scaffold's shape reminded Victor of a gallows, but that was just his nerves talking. He hoped.

Crude in comparison to the intricate workings of an actual Cataphract, the armature was the perfect thing for his thesis demonstration. The exposed gears and cabling of the armature allowed one to see how Victor had modified them specially for his project. While most of his effort had been centered on increasing the alchemical furnace's output, Victor had also taken the opportunity to adjust the gears and cabling, for maximum efficiency and leverage.

Victor saved the hardest point for last. Slowly, gingerly, he took hold of the control lever, testing the armature's responsiveness. The arm jerked to life in response, moving left, then right, up and down. Victor squeezed the single trigger mounted to the top of the control lever, and the arm's clamp of a hand opened and closed. Nervous sweat made the brass handle slick beneath Victor's hands; he was perfectly fine building or repairing such advanced machinery, but operating it was another matter entirely. Victor marveled to think of how a trained captain could operate a control lever in either hand while simultaneously working the movement pedals with their feet. It took all Victor's concentration to slowly swing the arm around without smashing it into the quarter-ton anvil sitting in the middle of the floor. His stomach turned when he thought about operating such a complicated machine in the middle of a battle.

"There you are!" Professor Dorrett's voice echoed through the otherwise-empty workshop. Victor managed not to jerk the control lever in response (if barely) and eased it into a locked, resting position before he turned to greet the faculty who would decide his fate. Doctor Waldwin and High Chemist Licelli followed Professor Dorrett, already sizing Victor up.

"Professors." Victor forced a smile and gave a polite bow, stepping in front of the most cluttered part of his workbench, just in case. "A pleasure, as always. If you would have a seat, I can get started." Victor gestured to the trio of chairs sitting just outside the reach of the armature. The chairs were the best furniture that could be found in the whole workshop, which meant that they were only slightly lopsided, and the cushions still had a bit of stuffing left.

"Wait." Doctor Waldwin held up a hand. "There will be a fourth observer judging you today."

"A fourth?" Victor's voice cracked.

"A fourth!" Professor Dorrett clapped Victor on the shoulder, hard enough to stagger him a step. "You haven't even graduated yet, and you're already getting noticed!"

"By who?" Victor wiped his suddenly sweaty palms off on his leather apron.

"By me." A deep, confident voice rolled through the workshop. Victor turned towards the sound, as did Professor Dorrett and the other masters. A tall man in a black, ermine-trimmed cape strode into the workshop. He carried himself with an aristocrat's confident swagger, chin tilted up as if to keep the tip of his meticulously trimmed goatee pointing forward like the prow of a sailing ship. The heels of his polished boots rapped sharply against the stone floor as he approached the group. Despite his fine attire, the man was entirely at ease among the tools, grease, and machinery of the university's workshop.

Victor's mouth went desert-dry as he saw the sigil embroidered in yellow thread on the left breast of the newcomer's doublet: a single coin, pierced by a long dagger. A Cataphract sigil. Only the Cataphract's captain would be allowed to wear such a badge. And there was only one man allowed to captain the *Guilt of Gold*.

"Marquis Maldrinne, it's an honor." Victor bowed deeply, keeping his eyes locked on the marquis' polished boots.

"I should hope so," the marquis said. "Now, please rise. Professor Dorrett told me some very interesting things about your theories, journeyman."

"He has?" Victor blurted as he stood up. "If I may so ask, just, er, how much did he tell you?"

"Enough." The marquis eased himself into the sturdiest-looking of the chairs, which thankfully didn't collapse beneath him. "Professor Dorrett's students have impressed me in the past--I hope you live up to their standard."

Professor Dorrett remained standing, allowing the other masters to claim the remaining seats. High Chemist Licielli took a small notebook and a stubby pencil out of her academic's robe, as if she were in a lecture hall and not sitting next to one of the most important men in the whole kingdom. "Whenever you're ready, Journeyman Brinden."

"Right. Whenever I'm ready. Which is right now. Because I'm ready. Now. Yes." Victor pushed his glasses further up his nose and stood up straight. He took in a deep breath, then launched into the speech he'd prepared.

"While the inner workings of the alchemical furnace are the foundation of Cataphract technology, and therefore human civilization, there is still much we don't understand. What we do know is that, when exposed to air, the unique crystalline structures within an alchemical furnace burn. Though 'burn' may not be the best term, given the fact that a properly maintained furnace can be used for centuries." A thought struck Victor, and he offered his potential patron a hopeful smile. "For example, marquis, the furnace within the *Guilt of Gold* dates back to the time of King Leopold the Canny, yes?"

Marquis Maldrinne leaned forward, causing his chair to squeak slightly. "That's correct."

Beside him, High Chemist Licielli jotted something down in her notebook.

Victor pressed on.

"The energy released by a lit alchemical furnace can be channeled into a Cataphract's motive gears, allowing it to move. Logically, a larger furnace is able to provide more power. In turn, a larger Cataphract is able to carry a larger alchemical furnace, the specificities of which are laid out in Sullustrom's Treatise on Alchemical Energy Exchange. Of course, this requires a larger furnace be available--it's said that the larger the furnace, the longer it takes to develop in the depths of the Kingsforge, but the crown has been understandably reluctant to share the exact details. However, in my studies, I began to wonder: is it possible to squeeze more power out of a smaller furnace?"

"How is it possible to surpass the natural perfection of the alchemical furnace?" Doctor Waldwin rasped. "What makes you think you're better than the brightest minds of the last four hundred years?"

"I don't think." Victor blinked as the words left his lips, then sputtered as he corrected himself. "I mean, ah, that is. I don't think that. That I'm better, that is. I wouldn't presume to think I could improve upon the elemental perfection of an alchemical furnace. That would be like saying I've mastered the tides, or the phases of the moon. But when I started looking at the surrounding components, I saw an opportunity."

Victor hunched over the alchemical furnace on his workbench, carefully turning the valves and knobs on the pipes surrounding it. "An alchemical furnace, for all its elemental perfection, is still reliant on its flame. In turn, flame requires air in order to burn. More air means a hotter flame, and a hotter flame means more power. Which is why I've attached this air pump to this alchemical furnace for the purpose of the demonstration." Victor pulled a switch, and an oiled-leather bellows connected to the alchemical furnace started pumping, moving up and down like the wheezing of some mechanical beast. The smoke trailing from the exhaust piping turned a thicker, darker blue as the furnace grew hotter.

"Typically, an alchemical furnace this small would only be a curiosity, too weak to even power a light skirmisher. However--" Victor pulled in a deep breath and then took hold of the control lever, gently easing the armature into motion. While he'd practiced with the armature before, he'd never done so for an audience, and soon found his palms sweating as a result.

Victor bit the inside of his cheek as he guided the clamp-hand to the loop of chain he'd left on the floor. He eased the clamp shut, then raised the arm. The chain went taut, lifting the large anvil precariously off the ground. The massive block of metal hung in midair, swaying ever so slightly, like the pendulum of an enormous clock.

"Impressive." The marquis looked over his shoulder at Professor Dorrett. "That's the second of your students to impress me, Dorrett. You have an eye for talent."

"Journeyman Brinden is one of my most talented pupils," Professor Dorrett noted with no small amount of pride.

"I can see why," said the marquis.

Victor smiled in relief. If the marquis was impressed, it almost didn't matter what the other masters thought. A position on the *Guilt of Gold*'s crew would be prestigious--not to mention well compensated. "After my modifications, even a simple training machine such as this one shows an exponential increase in--"

A short, sharp vibration rattled the control lever in Victor's hand. He clamped both hands around the handle to steady it and faked a smile.

"Is something wrong, journeyman?" Doctor Waldwin asked. High Chemist Licielli remained silent as she scribbled something down in her notebook. Behind them, Professor Dorrett winced but kept quiet. Victor was on his own.

"Nothing's wrong," Victor said with what he hoped sounded like confidence. "I'm just afraid I'm not nearly as skilled at handling Cataphracts as the esteemed marquis. If you would give me just a moment--" Another tremor ran up the length of the control lever. Victor clamped his teeth shut to keep himself from whimpering.

Despite his checklist, Victor knew he had missed something. Possibly two somethings. Two somethings that could turn into exponentially more somethings, at which point they'd cease to be individual "somethings" and collate into a collective disaster.

Victor hoped the masters hadn't noticed. Nobody was shouting at him, (not yet, at least) which meant there was still a chance he could muddle through his thesis presentation.

All Victor had to do was ease the anvil back to the floor, turn off the furnace, talk through the rest of the demonstration, and keep anyone from looking at his machinery too closely. So long as he could leave a good impression with the marquis, he could still earn a position working on one of the most impressive machines in the kingdom.

A third shock. This time it was accompanied by the resonant snap of a steel cable. Metal groaned and hardwood shattered as the armature collapsed, and the anvil crashed back down onto the stone floor. Links of chain and chips of stone cut through the air like angry wasps, and the enormous, skeletal arm swung in a wild arc, clipping Victor's shoulder hard enough to throw him to the ground.

Professor Dorrett and the other masters scattered, taking cover behind racks of tools and machinery. A plume of eye-stinging blue smoke roiled out of the pipes surrounding the alchemical furnace, clouding Victor's vision.

Frantic, Victor groped through the smoke, scalding his fingertips on a too-hot pipe before he found the shutoff valve. The shattered remnants of the armature went slack as Victor extinguished the alchemical furnace, and the broken, tangled mess of bent metal and splintered wood slumped to the floor. Victor took off his hat and waved it in front of his face, clearing the blue alchemical smoke from his eyes. By the time the smoke thinned out, wafting up towards the high ceiling above, the masters had emerged from their hiding places. The marquis, meanwhile, remained in his seat, unperturbed. Victor knew the marquis must have seen worse disasters out on the battlefield. The realization brought hope; if the marquis could see past Victor's failed experiment, see the underlying theory--

The marquis laughed. He held a gloved hand up to his mouth in the barest nod to politeness, even as his hearty laughter echoed from the workshop's high ceiling. "Turns out it was too good to be true. Better to know now. Just think, if someone let him loose on my *Guilt of Gold* ... " The marquis' laugh trailed off as he shook his head.

"On behalf of the university, I offer my apologies, marquis." High Chemist Licielli kept her voice even and polite. "Journeyman Brinden's failures are not indicative of the university as a whole. You may rest assured that he will not touch the *Guilt of Gold*--or any other Cataphract, for that manner."

"Are you sure?" The waxed tips of the marquis' mustache angled upwards as he smirked. "If the Brethren start acting up again, maybe we can just give them your student. Turn him loose on their Cataphracts and he'd have the war won in a day."

Victor opened his mouth to defend himself, but Doctor Waldwin held up a hand, silencing him. "Suffice it to say, marquis, if we had known Journeyman Brinden's demonstration would be this irresponsible--"

"Stop apologizing, you old goat. I've seen worse." The marquis stood, then dusted himself off. "If I were a lesser man, I'd have the boy flogged for wasting my time. But at least he was good for a laugh, hm? Now then, I have other matters to attend to, as do you. Shall we?"

Marquis Maldrinne strode out of the workshop, and the masters fell into step behind him.

As the group left, Victor realized they took with them any hope of his graduation, much less a prestigious commission afterward. He looked over his workbench, the complicated machineries mangled and twisted out of shape like battlefield casualties. And there, in the tangle of scattered tools and broken piping, was Victor's checklist, the checklist he'd gone over so many times before. He grabbed the slightly singed paper, looking over his notes for something he'd missed, anything to explain the disaster. There was only one box that hadn't been checked yet, at the very bottom of the page.

Clean up.

Victor sighed and picked up a broom.

CHAPTER 3

Alcohol wasn't on Victor's checklist, but it was the next logical step.

He ensconced himself at a corner table in a borderline-respectable tavern and tried to calm his jittery nerves with several pints of beer dark enough to chew on. As Victor drank, he leafed through his singed notes, searching for whatever he'd missed, whatever had ruined him. Somewhere between the second and third mug of beer, he found his mistake, and its sheer obviousness was enough to drive him to mugs number four and five.

"There you are, lad!"

Startled (and not particularly sober), Victor nearly spilled his drink, only for Professor Dorrett to catch the mug before it could tip over entirely. The older man pressed it back into Victor's hands, sat down in the chair across from him, and took a sip from his own drink. "You should've gone to the Bear and Hawk. Their beer's better."

Victor looked into his chipped ceramic mug. "I'll keep that in mind."

"Looks like you've been making good use of your time, though." Professor Dorrett surveyed the papers laid out on the table, alternately stained by dried blots of ink and fresh drops of ale. "So, what went wrong?"

"It was the bolts." Victor tapped the ink- and beer-stained diagram. "Why didn't I think of the bolts?"

"The bolts?" Professor Dorrett said. "Do tell."

Victor rubbed at the bridge of his nose. "I reinforced the cables and the motive gears, but not the bolts that held them to the scaffold. The armature was never designed for that kind of stress. All it took was for one of them to break, and then cascading, catastrophic failure." He laid a sketch of the modified armature out on the table and traced his finger from one point to the next, showing the order in which the bolts gave out. "And you know what the worst part is?"

"I imagine you're going to tell me." Professor Dorrett sat back.

"If I hadn't practiced as much as I did, I wouldn't have put as much stress on the bolts. They might have held for the demonstration. And then ... " Victor gulped down another mouthful of thick, room-temperature porter.

"And then you would've sheared a bolt on a proper Cataphract, instead of a training armature," Professor Dorrett said. "The marquis wouldn't be laughing then, let me tell you. Catastrophic failure like that is the sort of thing that could turn a battle, and then the next thing you know the Brethren have got a collar around your neck. So maybe it's for the best that you failed, hm? Experimentation, observation, repetition--all part of the process. It's not like you're the first journeyman to get a bit carried away in pursuit of a theory. Even Licielli and Waldwin will admit that."

"You've talked with the other masters?" Victor asked. "So I'm not--"

Professor Dorret held up a hand. "What happened today is my fault. Well, not the part where your experiment more or less exploded. But it was my idea to invite the marquis. I thought you'd leave an impression."

"Which I did." Victor groaned.

"Exactly," Professor Dorrett said. "If it had just been me and the other masters, well ... we could discuss your theory. That you've already identified the point of failure shows you're a clever lad. However, the marquis isn't an academic like you or I. He doesn't have a nuanced understanding of the experimental process. So where you and I see potential, he only sees failure. Unfortunately, Marquis Maldrinne is also somewhat ... influential."

"Which means no captain in all the kingdom will ever let me touch their Cataphract." Victor groaned and squinted into his frustratingly empty mug.

"Once again, your fundamental theory is sound, but you've overlooked a key point." Professor Dorrett waved at the apron-clad tavern keeper, who plunked a fresh pair of mugs down onto Victor's notes, exchanging them for the empty ones.

Victor tugged his notes out from under the mugs. "What did I miss?"

Professor Dorrett leaned in. "The marquis is a powerful and influential man. And one does not become so powerful and influential without making a few enemies."

"You don't mean the Brethren, do you?" Victor kept his voice low, conspiratorial, in case someone were to overhear the potentially treasonous line of conversation. "I could never--"

"Not them," Professor Dorrett said. "I'm talking about the marquis' personal enemies."

Victor sipped his beer and peered warily at the professor. "This sounds ... political."

"Everything's political, lad." Professor Dorrett leaned back in his chair, smug. "You're just too young to know it yet. Still, it's worth noting that noblemen such as the marquis--such as anyone well born enough to helm a Cataphract --are often headstrong. Contrarian, even. So if one particular aristocrat favors something, one of their rivals is sure to loathe it, just as a matter of principle. And, of course, the inverse is true."

"So you're saying that the marquis laughing at me is a good thing?"

"I don't know if I'd go that far. As again, it'd certainly be easier if your demonstration hadn't exploded at him, but there are still opportunities open to you. Or, specifically, an opportunity." Professor Dorrett took an envelope out of his robes and set it on a dry stretch of table. The red wax of the university's book-and-quill sigil sealing the envelope shut told Victor exactly what was inside.

A letter of recommendation.

Victor's heart pounded in his ears, loud enough that Professor Dorrett's voice sounded oddly distant. The young engineer clamped both his hands around his mug to keep himself from snatching the letter of recommendation off the table and focused on the professor's words.

"As it would happen, Count Fenvale, an old acquaintance of mine, is in need of an engineer. Also as it would happen, the count is no friend to Marquis Maldrinne. I honestly have tried to stay out of their feud, but this is probably your best option, given the circumstances."

Victor stared at the envelope. "So you've convinced the other masters to let me graduate, despite everything?"

"Not exactly, no." Professor Dorrett winced. "I kept them from failing you outright, but Waldwin thinks you need further study, and Licielli thinks you should do that studying somewhere else. Which is where this letter comes in. The count's estate is about two weeks' ride from here.

Pack up your books and your tools, and present yourself with this letter. Count Fenvale will be happy for the help. While you're working so far from the capital, Marquis Maldrinne and his ilk will forget about you and find something else to gossip about. Hopefully, by the time you finish, I'll be able to convince the other masters to give you a second chance at graduating."

Victor reached for the sealed letter, then stayed his hand before his fingertips could touch it. "Just what kind of project does the count need help with?"

"He didn't say. But don't worry, the count's not the sort who'd waste your talents building bridges or repairing mills. It's probably not tutoring, either. The count only has one daughter, and she's roughly your age, if I recall correctly. Whatever the count has planned, he needs a man of your particular skill set. He used to captain a Cataphract, so he knows what makes a good engineer."

Professor Dorrett set his mug down on the table and leaned forward, intently sizing Victor up. "So, what do you say, Victor? It might not be as prestigious or lucrative as serving crew for the *Guilt of Gold*, but it's the best option you've got. Unless, of course, you have some contingency plan I'm unaware of?"

"I, uh, don't. Have a contingency plan, that is. Or ... any plan, really. I'd been counting on ... not failing. Or at least not failing so catastrophically." Victor chewed at the inside of his cheek, then let himself pick the letter up, weighing the fine paper in his hand. "Thank you, professor."

"You're welcome, lad. Now then, drink up!" He clinked his mug against Victor's. "To opportunity!"

The alchemical furnace was the most important discovery of the Behemoth Age, and the Cataphracts powered by those furnaces were the most impressive. However, the most practical invention of that bygone era had to be the Cataphract roads. Wide, level, and built from alchemically treated stone, the Cataphract roads were specifically engineered to withstand the tread of multiton war machines. The roads allowed even the heaviest siegebreakers to cross the kingdom without getting bogged down in a muddy field or sunk in a river. Centuries after they'd been laid out, the network of massive roads and bridges still endured, even if they were used more by travelers and merchants than marching Cataphracts. An informal hierarchy had developed around the old roads; one could get a rough approximation of a noble's social and financial standing by how close their home was to the network. In the old days, this was an indication of the particular noble's readiness to march out and face a marauding Behemoth or invading army. But in the modern era, the aristocracy mostly appreciated having easy access to the luxuries, news, and visitors that came with passing merchants.

Fenvale Manor was three days' ride from the nearest Cataphract road.

With the aid of a map Professor Dorrett had given him, along with the guidance of the occasional peasant, Victor navigated from one small farming village to the next, making his way steadily towards Fenvale Manor. As he neared his destination, the villages got further and further apart, and the forests between them grew deeper and wilder. According to the directions Professor Dorrett had provided, Fenvale Manor sat atop a hill overlooking a damp and muddy stretch of forest.

Victor's gray-maned mare plodded up over narrow roads, and the pack mule carrying his books, tools, and alchemical reagents kept pace behind. Not a particularly fast pace, Victor reflected, but any progress was better than no progress at all. At least he'd had the foresight to buy a mule, rather than a cart. Anything with wheels would have sunk down to the axles in short order, which would have slowed Victor even more.

In the distance, the setting sun silhouetted the pointed roof of a stone tower, jutting up over the treeline at the top of the hill: Fenvale Manor. Encouraged by the prospect of a warm meal and a proper bed after so long on the road, Victor spurred his horse onward. By his rough estimate, Victor figured he could make it to the manor house before dark so long as nothing interrupted him.

About halfway up the hill, something did.

Victor heard a rumbling first, coming from somewhere behind. Thunder--no, hoofbeats, Victor realized. Fast ones. He turned around in his saddle and saw four riders bearing down on him. Upon catching sight of Victor, the lead rider took off his hat and waved it above his head. "Ho there! Wait!" Waning sunlight glinted from the hilts of the sabers and horse pistols hanging from their saddles. Victor noted the fine cut of their clothing, which either meant they weren't bandits, or that they were very successful ones.

Victor reined his mare to a halt, knowing full well the old horse couldn't outrun the trained riders, much less with the pack mule following behind. "Uh, hello?" he ventured.

"Well met, friend!" The lead rider, hard-faced but smiling, put his hat back on as he brought his own horse up beside Victor's. Everything about the man was big: his beard, his muscles, his personality. As he spoke, his deep voice struck Victor in the chest like the thrum of heavy machinery. "You're heading for the count's manor, yes?"

"That's correct." Victor spared a glance over his shoulder as the other horsemen arrayed themselves in a loose circle around him. "How did you know?"

"That's the only place this sorry excuse for a road leads, friend. But I forget myself--my name is Rochen Dunsall." The enormous rider smiled broadly.

"Victor Brinden."

"A pleasure! Now then, Victor--if you would be so kind, please allow us to escort you."

"To Fenvale Manor?"

"To someplace more suited to a gentleman such as yourself."

"Thank you for the invitation, but I have urgent business with the count." To prove his point, Victor took his letter of recommendation from inside his doublet and showed the red wax seal of the university to Dunsall.

"Ah." The big man's smile grew tighter, less friendly, and he laid a gloved hand upon the brass-wrapped hilt of his saber. "My apologies, friend. I wasn't clear. When I said my associates and I were going to escort you, it was not a request."

"Oh." Victor swallowed despite the sudden desert-dryness of his mouth. "I--I just want you to know that if it's money you want, I'm afraid I don't have enough to be worth your while."

"Let me be the judge of that, friend," Dunsall said, "After all, that letter alone implies you're a gentleman of some import. That, and I wonder what's important enough to haul all the way up this damn hill." Rochen nodded curtly at one of his men, and the well-armed rider dismounted. He

23

slid a long dagger out of its scabbard as he walked over to the pack mule, then cut a hole in one of the tightly packed bundles strapped to the mule's back.

"Careful!" Victor blurted. He turned in his saddle and watched in horror as the horseman pulled out random books and tools, examined them for a moment, then tossed them over his shoulder when they proved uninteresting. "Most of my equipment is quite delicate--"

"Delicate?" Rochen laughed. "Now we're onto something, friend. Delicate means valuable."

Victor winced. "Not necessarily? I mean, it's not as if you can just sell an alchemical thaumic gauge at a pawn shop."

"Mmm. Specialized, then. Specialized also can mean valuable. To the right people." Dunsall shrugged. "The question is, should my associates rummage through your delicate, specialized equipment on this rough and muddy road, or should we relocate to someplace more appropriate?"

"I'll go with you. Just be careful. That man's liable to burn his hands off, at this rate."

The man rummaging through Victor's baggage immediately stepped back, dropping a copy of Principles of Ambulatory Motion into the mud.

"You've booby-trapped your own belongings?" Rochen's tone hovered somewhere between wary and impressed.

"Not as such, no. But there's a reason I've got the mule on such a long lead. As an alchemical engineer, my work often requires the use of certain reagents and mixtures that can be ... caustic. Or poisonous. Or explosive. Or possibly all three, if handled incorrectly."

"Why in blazes would you carry something that dangerous?"

"Because I can handle the components correctly," Victor noted.

"So we're safe at this distance?"

"We're safer at this distance. If your associate keeps on like that, he's likely to set the whole forest on fire, at which point we'll be lucky if we choke to death on the smoke before we're roasted alive."

"You make a compelling point." Rochen drew his saber in a

practiced, smooth motion. Victor flinched away from the polished blade, and the huge man laughed.

"Relax. This isn't for you, friend. And it won't be, so long as you're sensible." Rochen leaned over and neatly slashed through the rope hanging from the back of Victor's saddle. "Leave the mule!"

At the order, the highwayman nodded gratefully and remounted his horse, keeping a wary distance from Victor's mule. Rochen rested his saber against his shoulder and turned his attention back to Victor. "I must say, friend, that I appreciate your honesty. A more devious man might have tried talking me into allowing him to unpack the volatiles himself and used them as a weapon. Which would not have ended well for anyone involved. Now then, if you would be so kind as to follow me?" Rochen walked his horse past Victor, away from Fenvale Manor. "I presume you'll be smart enough not to try running. I'd hate to have to shoot you."

"I'll keep that in mind." Victor clutched his reins in sweaty palms and guided his horse to follow. They gave Victor's mule a wide berth, then fell into formation with Victor at the center. Under different circumstances, one could have taken the four highwaymen for an honor guard. The precision of their formation was enough to make Victor feel sloppy and undisciplined in comparison. Rochen slid his saber back into its scabbard, though the men on either side of Victor kept their hands distressingly close to their weapons.

They rode about a quarter of a mile before the pounding of hoofbeats echoed from behind them, further up the hill. For a moment, Victor wondered if it was his pack mule, only to realize that he'd never seen the stubborn thing move that fast.

No sooner had Victor reached that conclusion, a rider in a billowing cloak, mounted on a white horse, came into view. The stranger charged straight for them, drawing a long saber. Steel flashed in the waning sunlight, and the highwayman behind Victor cried out as he fell from his saddle. Rochen's men went for their swords and pistols, but the stranger plunged straight in among them, blade flashing. The man at Victor's side leaned forward in his saddle for a scything slash, only for the rider to neatly parry the blow and cut deeply into the highwayman's arm on the backswing. Knowing he'd never get a better opening, Victor pulled his mare's reins to the side, preparing to gallop off into the forest.

"Not so fast, friend!" Rochen Dunsall swung his horse around to block Victor's path. There was no warmth behind the big man's smile as he thumbed back the hammer of one of his horse pistols. Victor stared down the cavernously large barrel, mouth flapping open and closed as he tried to wordlessly beg for his life.

Before Rochen could fire, a snarling brown blur burst out of the treeline and pounced upon him. The beast closed its massive, white-fanged jaws on Rochen's gun arm, then dragged the big man down and out of his saddle. Rochen swore as he grappled with the creature, which, from what Victor could see, appeared to be some sort of enormous dog, or possibly a small and acrobatic bear.

Man and beast rolled over each other, and Victor's mare whinnied and shied away from the fighting. Victor wheeled his horse about, searching for another escape route, only to find himself face-to-face with the rider attacking them. The hood of the rider's cloak had fallen back in the melee, revealing a young woman's face. Her complexion was a light brown in color, her features sharp and aristocratic, her eyes hard and canny. Behind her, Rochen's men lay on the ground, groaning and clutching at fresh wounds. The woman flicked blood from her saber and looked past Victor.

"Lily, hold!" she shouted.

The dog-beast wrestling with Rochen stopped growling but kept her jaws clamped around his arm. The woman walked her horse past Victor and loomed over Rochen. "You're a long way from home, Dunsall," she said flatly.

"Damn you, woman, call the bitch off!" Rochen swore.

"I've already kept her from tearing your throat out."

"What do you want?" Rochen asked through gritted teeth.

"I want you to tell my cousin I don't appreciate his men waylaying my guests. Note that I haven't killed any of you, for politeness' sake." The woman's blade flashed, neatly slicing a corner off Rochen's cape. She speared the scrap of fabric with her sword, then sat up straight in her saddle as she used the rag to wipe the blood from her blade. "Next time, I may not be so merciful."

"Next time, I'll bring a whole squadron." Rochen sneered.

"I hope you do. Lily could use the exercise." The woman tossed the bloodied rag away, then put her free hand to her mouth and whistled

26

sharply. The hulking dog immediately released Rochen's arm and obediently trotted over to stand beside the swordswoman's horse. "But for now, I'm going to let you go. You're a smart man, Dunsall. Don't waste this opportunity."

"I won't." Rochen picked his hat up off the ground as he slowly, painfully got to his feet.

"Good. Now go." The woman pointed down the road with her saber. "And leave your blades. I'm adding them to my collection."

Rochen grumbled, but unsheathed his sword and tossed it to the muddy ground before he clambered back into the saddle. The rest of his men did the same, muttering and swearing beneath their breath. Soon, they spurred their horses on, heading back down the hill and into the forest. The woman watched them leave and only sheathed her saber several minutes after Rochen and his men disappeared from view. As the woman relaxed, so did her dog. Lily turned her broad, blocky head to peer curiously at Victor, staring at him with amber eyes that shone with more intelligence than he was particularly comfortable with.

"You must be Victor Brinden," the woman said.

"That's me, yes. How did you know?" Victor asked. As far as he was aware, Professor Dorrett hadn't sent word ahead of him.

"I found this further up the trail." She took a mud-stained copy of Manx's Principles of Ambulatory Motion out of her cloak and tossed it to Victor. "Your name's on the bookplate."

"Thank you." Victor fumbled to catch the book and just barely managed not to drop it or fall out of the saddle in the process. "For returning the book. And for saving my life, as well. But, er, would you be so kind as to tell me your name, so I can thank you more, ah, specifically?"

"You may call me Lady Fenvale."

CHAPTER 4

A blocky structure of heavy stone and timber, Fenvale Manor had the air of a fortress, made more imposing by the evening's long shadows. Though if Fenvale Manor was a fortress, it was an undermanned one. The only soul visible was a gaunt old man standing in front of the house's main door with a lantern in his hand and a brace of pistols in his belt.

He raised the lantern as Lady Fenvale rode up to the manor house. "A good night's hunting, Madam?"

"I'd say so, Turquo." Lady Fenvale tossed a bundle of captured swords to the ground with a clatter. She swung out of her saddle, then crouched down to ruffle Lily's ears. "It'll be a long while before Dunsall lifts a sword again. Longer still before he lifts one against us, for that matter."

"Very good, your Ladyship." Turquo nodded, then looked over at Victor. "And we have a guest?"

"We do." Lady Fenvale stood up, then handed her horse's reins to the old man. "This is Victor Brinden. He's from the university."

"Is he?" Turquo said.

"I am, yes. Er--from the university, that is," Victor said as he dismounted. While clumsier in his movements than Lady Fenvale, he didn't fall on his face, which he counted as something of an accomplishment. Victor took his letter of recommendation out of his pocket and presented it to Turquo. "Professor Dorrett instructed me to give this to the count."

Turquo took the reins of Victor's mount, but left him holding the slightly crumpled but still sealed envelope. "I'm afraid the His Lordship has already retired for the evening."

"I'll introduce him tomorrow, then." Lady Fenvale plucked the letter out of Victor's hand before he could protest. "In the meanwhile, I could do with a drink."

"I've already prepared refreshments. You'll find them in the main hall," Turquo said. "If you need anything more substantial, I shall be happy to assist once I've stabled the horses."

"Whatever you've put together, I'm sure it will be delicious,

Turquo." Lady Fenvale smiled and patted the old man affectionately on the shoulder before she pushed the heavy oak door open. Lily wagged her whiplike tail and bumped Victor with her bulky shoulder as she trotted past him to take her place beside Lady Fenvale.

Victor kept his footing (if barely) and looked to Turquo as the old man started leading the horses and the pack mule away.

"Er--Turquo, was it?"

"Sir?" The old man stopped.

"Perhaps it would be best if I were to help you unload that mule. There are certain items in my baggage that are somewhat ... delicate. Even volatile."

"No need, sir. I'm familiar with your profession." Turquo nodded. "I presume you've brought your own etching acids. Are you using the Ridley formula, or the Margini?"

"The Ridley," Victor said, blinking.

"Then I shall take the proper precautions and make sure I have a bucket of sand close by. Thank you for the warning, sir." Turquo bowed his head, then led the mounts out of sight behind the manor house.

"Turquo was my father's staff sergeant," Lady Fenvale said. "He's not an engineer himself, but he's seen enough to know how not to break anything. Now come on, I'm thirsty."

Victor followed the swordswoman inside. Fenvale Manor was better lit inside than out, mostly on account of the blazing hearth on the far side of the main hall. Smells of woodsmoke and dust wafted through the air, ancient and inviting at the same time. At least the furniture looked comfortable enough, with several old but plush couches and chairs pulled up into a semicircle near the fireplace.

A low table sat in the middle of the couches, with a platter of bread, cheese, and dry sausage laid out next to a tall bottle of wine. The arranged furniture and refreshments were incongruously intimate in the large hall. The room had obviously been built to receive dozens of visitors at a time. Or possibly repel them, to judge from the amount of cutlery hanging from the walls. From the way the firelight shone from the polished steel, it was obvious the weapons were more practical than ornamental. Victor wondered how many of those swords Lady Fenvale had collected

29

personally.

Lady Fenvale took off her cloak and sword belt and tossed both onto one of the empty couches. Beneath the cloak, she wore a simple, matched set of doublet and trousers. That she wore men's clothing didn't surprise Victor so much as the fact that she wore such plain clothing. After the swordswoman's earlier performance, he'd almost expected her to have gilded armor hidden beneath her cloak. She stood taller than Victor (who himself wasn't exactly a short man), and her baggy clothing couldn't completely hide the honed muscle of her arms and shoulders.

Lily hunkered down on the floor beside Lady Fenvale, the dog's bulk nearly the size of the couch. Victor sat down on the other side of the low table and tried not to sink too deeply into the couch's surprisingly plush cushions. Lady Fenvale poured out two glasses of dark red wine. They clinked glasses for politeness' sake, and Lady Fenvale drained most of hers in a single, thirsty gulp. Victor drank his glass more slowly, allowing the dry wine to calm his rattled nerves.

Lady Fenvale picked up a coin-shaped chunk of sausage and tossed it to Lily. The big dog snapped the sausage out of the air, teeth slamming together like a spring-loaded trap.

"That is the biggest dog I've ever seen." Victor watched the play of thick muscles beneath Lily's short brown coat. "She ... is a dog, yes?"

"Lily is a hackleback mastiff." Lady Fenvale tossed another piece of sausage to her dog, who happily scarfed it down.

"I haven't heard of the breed." Victor ate a bite-sized piece of sharp yellow cheese.

"They're rare. Hackleback mastiffs were originally bred to track and harry Behemoths. Seeing as there aren't very many Behemoths to hunt anymore, she makes do with bandits and highwaymen." Lady Fenvale's smile softened as she reached over and ruffled Lily's floppy ears. "She's a good girl." The big dog basked in the attention.

"She saved my life." As soon as he said the words, Victor realized just how dry his mouth was. He finished his glass, then looked up at the young woman sitting across from him. "You saved my life, Lady Fenvale. Thank you."

"Think nothing of it. Dunsall and his men have been trespassing far too often of late. It was a pleasure to finally send them running."

"Do you usually have, uh ... bandit problems?"

"Those men weren't bandits. They're in my cousin's employ."

"Your cousin?"

"Marquis Maldrinne."

Victor choked on his wine.

"So you've heard of him," Lady Fenvale said.

Victor thumped himself on the chest, then forced a nervous smile once he could breathe again. "Who hasn't?"

"Point." Lady Fenvale topped off Victor's glass.

"Why? Why would your cousin armed raiders after you?" Victor asked.

"The marquis thinks he has a claim to my father's estate. He's too much of a coward to face us openly, so he sends his lackeys to harass anyone who strays too far from the Cataphract road. He thinks if he can isolate my father and me from the rest of the kingdom, we'll capitulate. Lily and I have fended the bastards off without much trouble, but it will ... complicate things, once my cousin finds out an alchemic engineer is visiting." Lady Fenvale paused, eyed Victor from over the rim of her wineglass. "Let's hope you're worth it."

"About that--" Victor began.

Lady Fenvale held up a hand. "I know Fenvale Manor has seen better days, but you may rest assured that you'll be fairly compensated for your work."

"I never had any doubt," Victor said, even as he realized that Professor Dorrett hadn't mentioned monetary compensation when describing the opportunity. Suddenly hungry, he started assembling a sandwich from the cuts of meat and cheese on the table. "It's just ... well, it would help if I knew exactly what you need an alchemic engineer for, exactly?"

"My father--the count--should be the one to tell you. It's his plan." Lady Fenvale tossed another piece of sausage to her dog, who easily snapped it out of the air before the cured meat could hit the floor. "I won't tell you anything before he does. The last thing I want to do is give you wrong information by accident."

"That's sensible." Victor nodded.

"In the meanwhile, you must be exhausted after all you've been through. Turquo, show our guest to his room."

"Of course, my lady." Turquo spoke from a point directly behind Victor.

The surprise made Victor choke on his wine again. Once he finished wheezing, he looked over his shoulder and marveled at how silently the old valet had appeared.

"Whenever you're ready, sir." Turquo's expression remained politely blank.

"Ah. Sleep. Yes." Victor stood, then winced as the last few weeks' ride caught up with him and set his legs to aching. "And, er--thank you again, Lady Fenvale."

"You can thank me by helping my father."

"I shall do my best." Victor bowed, if stiffly.

Lady Fenvale leaned over and scratched Lily behind the ears. "Let's hope so."

CHAPTER 5

Victor woke at dawn, through no fault of his own.

The guest room's narrow windows faced east, and the bed was positioned at just the right angle to allow the first rays of the sunrise to beam directly into the sleeper's face in a manner that had to be intentional. Dark as it had been the night before, Victor hadn't noticed the positioning of the bed relative to the window. Despite this, the guest room still surpassed the students' hostel he'd lived in during his time at the university (to say nothing of the various roadside inns and taverns he'd been sleeping in for the last few weeks). It was bigger, more comfortably furnished, and featured a decided lack of other students staggering home in the dark and drunken hours of the morning.

Victor rolled out of bed, rubbed the sleep from his eyes, and picked his glasses up from where he'd left them on the nightstand. The small trunk containing his meager wardrobe sat in a corner. Victor wondered how long it had been there. He could have simply not noticed it the night before, though it was equally plausible Turquo had silently put it in place while Victor was asleep. Either way, Victor was relieved to have something less travel-stained to wear. He changed into a fresh set of clothing, buckled his boots, and stepped out into the hall.

By daylight, Fenvale Manor was slightly less imposing. Motes of dust floated through the morning sunlight as a reminder of the house's emptiness. Unused furniture had been shoved into odd corners and covered with canvas to keep the dust off, which gave them the look of small, lumpy mountains. Oil paintings of Fenvales past lined the hallways' walls (at least where various arms weren't kept within easy reach). The portraits showed men and women with similar sharp-featured faces and stern expressions. Victor paused in front of one of the larger paintings, one of a broad-shouldered man in a maroon jacket and black sword belt. The man in the painting had the image of a leaping hound stitched into his jacket over his left breast: a Cataphract's sigil. Victor wracked his brain, trying to remember which Cataphract the leaping-hound sigil belonged to, but sleep still clouded his mind.

"Count Fenvale, in better times," Turquo said from behind Victor. "It's a Gustovus original."

Victor turned around, thankful he wasn't carrying anything to spill all over himself in surprise. "It's--it's quite impressive. The painting, that is.

33

As is the count himself, I'm sure."

"You may judge that for yourself," Turquo said. "The count requests your company at breakfast."

Victor barely recognized the man sitting at the head of the long table as the same man from the portrait. He wore the same maroon jacket with the same leaping-hound sigil stitched over the breast, but his clothes hung loosely from his age-eroded frame. The dark hair from the painting had faded to silver, and countless wrinkles creased his face. But for all his aging, the count's eyes still had the same piercing intensity that Gustovus captured so well in the official portrait: an intensity that was directed at Victor as soon as he walked in the room. Sitting to the count's right, dressed in a jacket of the same color (but better fit), Lady Fenvale regarded him with the same scrutiny. Even Lily, sitting on the floor at Lady Fenvale's right, had a serious look on her muzzle, though her eyes were locked on the toast and pork belly laid out on the table.

"Er--Good morning, your Lordship," Victor said after a moment, unsure of the proper protocol. A moment after that, he made a polite (if awkward) bow. "My name is Victor--"

"Victor Brinden, yes." The count spoke with a gravelly rasp. "I don't like discussing business on an empty stomach. Sit. Eat."

"Thank you, your Lordship." Victor eased himself into an empty chair across from Lady Fenvale, then helped himself to breakfast. The pork belly was heavily salted, but Turquo soon provided a mug of steaming tea to wash it down. Victor ate politely and tried not to flinch whenever Lady Fenvale tossed a morsel into Lily's spring trap of a mouth. Count Fenvale watched the display with a father's affection, as if Lady Fenvale were a small girl spoiling her puppy, instead of a grown woman encouraging a hulking war beast of a dog. Lily made short work of whatever scraps she got and thumped her tail on the hardwood floor so vigorously that Victor could feel it through his boots on the other side of the table.

"So," Count Fenvale said. "My daughter tells me you had some trouble coming in."

Victor occupied his hands by spreading a smear of butter across his toast. "That's correct, yes. Thankfully, your daughter arrived before things

34

could get out of control."

"Things have been out of control for years now. That useless fop of a marquis can't even wait till I'm dead. Bah." Count Fenvale stabbed a chunk of pork belly with the point of his knife.

"I don't understand," Victor said. "If you die, won't your titles and estate go to your daughter?"

"That'd be the logical thing, wouldn't it?" Count Fenvale grumbled. "Diana--Lady Fenvale--is worth a dozen mewling brats like Maldrinne. But since she's a woman, she's not allowed to inherit, per the family charter. So when I die, the marquis will claim my lands, my title, and everything that comes with it. I can thank my idiot grandfather for that. He's the one who laid out the terms with the crown."

"You could have remarried after mother died," Lady Fenvale said.

"And you could have--" Count Fenvale trailed off into a rasping cough.

Lady Fenvale set a hand on her father's shoulder. "Perhaps you should--"

"I'm fine, Diana." The count shrugged off Lady Fenvale's hand. He gulped down a mouthful of tea, then pulled in a long, steadying breath. "Or at least as fine as I can be in my old age. I just need some fresh air, that's all."

Count Fenvale got to his feet, though it was a slow process. He snapped his fingers, at which point Turquo picked up a brass-handled cane from where it had been left lying against the wall and handed it to him. Lady Fenvale stood and moved to help him, but the count waved her off. "I think that's enough breakfast," the count said, "Let's show Mister Brinden just what he's here for."

Slowly, but with no assistance from anyone else, Count Fenvale led them out of the dining room, through the manor's rear door, and across a grass-patched field. The two-story carriage house shared the same solid block-and-timber construction of the rest of the manor, as did the mostly empty stables branching off from its left side.

Turquo picked up his pace, walking past Count Fenvale so he could open up the carriage house's tall, heavy doors. Iron hinges creaked as the doors opened, revealing a large, dirt-floored room. Victor's tools and books had been neatly unpacked and arranged on a long workbench on one side, while various crates and cloth bundles sat piled up against the opposite wall. Heavy ropes hung from heavier pulleys set in the rafters, and Victor even saw a small forge and bellows set up in the corner. It was everything one needed to work on a Cataphract.

Including the Cataphract itself.

Even kneeling and hunched over, the machine took up most of the space in the carriage house. A sail-sized canvas had been draped over it, as if it were just another forgotten piece of furniture. Even still, the disguise was a flimsy one. Metal plating glinted from worn holes in the old fabric, and there was no concealing the shape, the scale of a duelist-class Cataphract.

"Well, go on." Count Fenvale nudged Victor forward. "Take a look."

Needing no further prompting, Victor walked across the dirt floor to stand in front of the Cataphract. Slowly, reverently, he pulled the canvas aside to reveal an image etched into the white-enameled metal of the Cataphract's breastplate. Victor stared at the picture of a hunting dog, frozen mid-leap, and it all came together.

"It's the *Huntress*." Victor ran his fingers over the cool, tarnished steel.

"What's left of her, at least," Count Fenvale said.

"What's left of--what happened?"

"Osterbridge."

"I was there. I saw the *Huntress*--I saw you fight off the whole Brethren army."

"And my nephew never forgave me for it." Count Fenvale spat on the dirt floor.

"What?" Victor blinked.

"I showed him up." Count Fenvale rasped out a rueful laugh. "And I didn't even have the courtesy to die from my wounds afterward like a hero should. So once things had settled, Maldrinne bribed a team of engineers to declare *Huntress* irreparable. And once that verdict went out, I couldn't get the money or the backing to repair her. Not right away, at least."

36

The count limped over to the supplies piled on the far wall and rapped his knuckles on one of the crates. "I spent the last few years stockpiling everything needed to get *Huntress* up and running again. Tools. Parts. Materials. And now, Victor Brinden, you."

"So that's the project." Victor chewed at the inside of his cheek as he looked up at the canvas-shrouded *Huntress* looming far above him. "You want me to repair the *Huntress*. By myself. In an improvised workshop, using only whatever equipment and materials you've been able to scrounge up."

"It's not too much for you, is it?" Lady Fenvale asked, no small amount of challenge in her voice.

Victor rubbed his hands together. "When can I start?"

CHAPTER 6

"I need more paper," Victor said.

Lady Fenvale scowled. "It's been nearly a week, and that's all you have to say?"

"It took me two days to build the scaffolding." Victor gestured to the mostly stable network of ladders and planks he had set up around the *Huntress* so he could access any part of the massive machine. "Another two to catalog the *Huntress*' condition, and one more to inventory the supplies your father has graciously provided. And now that I've taken that inventory, I've found that I'm going to need more paper. The larger the sheets, the better. It takes a lot of room to lay out the diagrams in any kind of useful scale."

"If I wanted someone to draw me a picture, I would've hired an artist." She looked up at the *Huntress*, stripped of the canvas shroud. The Cataphract's once-gleaming armor was scuffed and dusty, marred by large dents in a dozen places.

"Every Cataphract has--or should have a proper diagram. Something to show how it's been built and what modifications have been done to it over the years. Unfortunately, the *Huntress*' schema and repair logs were lost after Osterbridge. At least, that's what Turquo told me. It makes sense. If Marquis Maldrinne wanted to sabotage the repair effort, getting rid of those would be an easy way to do it."

"And you can't fix the *Huntress* without them?"

"I didn't say that. But if I just plunge in and start taking out broken parts without understanding how to install new ones, I could break something, and all this effort would be wasted. Think of the diagrams like a map. Without one, I'd just be blundering around without any idea of my destination. But, if I take the time to chart a course beforehand, it could prevent disaster later. Does that make sense?"

"Somewhat." Lady Fenvale crossed her arms over her chest.

"I assure you, I'm doing everything I can to get the *Huntress* up and running again, as soon as feasibly possible. I just want to make sure I do it properly. Though the good news is, I should be able to repair most of the damage without too much trouble."

Lady Fenvale narrowed her eyes. "Most?"

"Yes, well. Some of the outer armor will need to be replaced. I can fashion new plating from what we've got on hand. Likewise, if any of the control cables are broken, I should be able to splice them without much trouble--though, honestly, it might be better if I just put in new ones."

"Then what's the trouble?"

"The exhaust vents are half-slagged. I'll have to run a vapor test to see if they've been blocked completely."

"So replace them."

"It's not that easy. The exhaust pipes are directly linked to the alchemical furnace, the literal heart of the Cataphract. In order to access those mechanisms, I'll have to remove all the other components blocking access. And in order to do that, I'll need to keep proper notes so I can reassemble everything correctly once I'm done. And in order to do that, I'll need something to write on."

Lady Fenvale pressed her lips into a thin line. "I'll tell Turquo to find some paper for you."

"Thank you," Victor said. "Though on the upside, we have something of an opportunity. If I have to dig that deep into the *Huntress*, I can take the opportunity to make certain improvements."

"Oh?" Lady Fenvale looked at Victor with renewed interest. "What kind of improvements?"

"At the university, I wrote my thesis on methods to make the processes of an alchemical furnace more efficient--which in turn would have a marked effect on the Cataphract's performance. Admittedly, there are a few minor difficulties to be worked out." Victor winced inwardly as he remembered his disastrous thesis presentation, which already seemed as if it had taken place years before, instead of weeks. "But I assure you--"

"Do it."

"Are you sure? You don't need to consult the count first?"

"My father trusts my judgment, and I shall trust yours." Lady Fenvale walked across the carriage house and ran her palm over the metal of the *Huntress'* foot. "Besides, I don't want to restore the *Huntress* to her former glory. She needs to be better than what she was. We will need every possible advantage in the days ahead. So if there's anything you can do to make her stronger, faster, tougher, you are to do it. Do you understand?"

"Absolutely." Victor jotted down "double-check structural bolts" in the margins of one of his notebooks. "Though, a question. Just who's going to be operating the *Huntress* once I have her up and running?"

"My father, obviously," Lady Fenvale said. "Or, if he is indisposed, I can take the helm."

"You?" Victor blurted.

"When I was a little girl, my father let me sit in his lap when he took the *Huntress* on parade. He told me exactly what each lever and gauge was for, and I can still recite the layout from memory." Lady Fenvale looked up at the dormant machine and sighed softly. When she turned back to Victor, her tone grew sterner, more challenging. "When I got older, I trained on the same armatures that all the other candidates did. Or did you think I'm not capable simply because I'm a--"

Outside, Lily barked.

Lady Fenvale stiffened. "Someone's here. Follow me, and secure the door behind you." She pushed past Victor, grabbing her sword belt from where she'd left it hanging by the door. Victor hustled to follow and squinted as the early afternoon glare hit his eyes. He pulled the heavy carriage house door closed behind him, while Lady Fenvale buckled on her saber without breaking stride. Lily barked again, a deep, booming sound that echoed across the hilltop.

Victor and Lady Fenvale rounded the corner, where they saw Lily standing resolutely in front of Fenvale Manor's front door. She barked again, growling low in her chest. Behind her stood Turquo, unflappable as always. The both of them stared down none other than Rochen Dunsall as he pulled on his horse's reins, trying to keep the black gelding from bolting away from Lily's fearsome presence. Lady Fenvale took up a position alongside her dog, while Victor wound up standing beside Turquo.

"Where's your squadron, Dunsall?" Lady Fenvale dragged her thumb over the brass pommel of her saber "Or did you grow a spine when I wasn't looking?"

"You wound me, Lady Fenvale." Rochen finally got his horse

under control.

"As I recall, it was Lily who had that honor." She nodded to the white bandages wrapped around Rochen's right arm. "Now, give me a reason I shouldn't turn her loose so she can do it again."

The big dog licked her lips.

"I come bearing news," Rochen said.

"Then speak. Quickly."

"Marquis Maldrinne is hosting a Summer's Steel festival at his country estate to celebrate the grand history of Leovaix. Something a little less formal than the celebrations at the capital itself, but sure to be the event of the season." Dunsall dismounted, then took a sealed white envelope from his horse's saddlebags. "The marquis has already made arrangements for the finest food, drink, and entertainment for his guests to enjoy. There's even talk he's commissioned none other than Carondel himself to write a play for his guests' amusement. Something about the Fourth Regent, if rumor's to be believed.

"It is my pleasure to convey the marquis' invitation. Although, given your father's ... condition, the marquis understands if you are unable to attend." Rochen took a step closer to present the letter, then thought the better of it as Lily gave another low growl. Turquo wordlessly walked forward, bowed to Rochen, and received the envelope with both hands. This done, he turned around and presented the envelope to Lady Fenvale with an even deeper bow.

Lady Fenvale took the letter from her servant, but didn't open it. "My father's condition is no business of yours. Or my cousin's, for that matter."

"I never said it was." Dunsall smiled a polite smile, though it didn't reach his eyes. "Count Fenvale must be a busy man, if he wasn't able to come out and greet me himself."

"My father has better things to do than greet every rogue and vagabond that comes calling."

"So he has his daughter speak to them instead? That verges on the scandalous."

"And your words verge on insulting." Lady Fenvale's fingers tightened around her sword hilt.

41

"I meant no disrespect, my lady." Rochen took a step back, just in case. "Even though our last encounter was ... less than amicable, please understand that I bear you no ill will. Nor does your cousin, the marquis--as is evidenced by his invitation."

Lady Fenvale scowled.

"In any case." Rochen put his boot to his horse's stirrup and swung his other leg up over the saddle in an easy, practiced motion. "I'd best be going, before that dog of yours tries to eat my horse. Until next time, Lady Fenvale." Rochen tipped his hat, then turned his mount around and started down the hill. Lily let out a derisive snort, then scratched herself behind the ear with her back paw.

"Turquo." Lady Fenvale spoke a few minutes after Dunsall disappeared from view. "Take Lily and make a patrol of the grounds. Make sure Dunsall hasn't tried to sneak any of his lackeys in while he distracted us. Once you're done, meet me in my father's chambers."

"Of course, my lady." Turquo bowed and set off towards the tree line. He whistled a short command, and Lily bounded after him, tail wagging.

"Ah. Lady Fenvale?" Victor spoke up. "Is there anything you'd like me to do?"

Lady Fenvale closed her eyes and breathed in deeply, steadying herself. "My cousin's party is less than a month away, Victor."

"That is correct, yes."

"The *Huntress* is to be operational by then."

Victor ran some brief calculations in his head. "It's theoretically possible. But that wouldn't leave much time to spare--"

"Which is why I suggest you get started."

Victor redoubled his efforts. The work went faster once he finished his basic schematics of the *Huntress'* components. Each day, Victor woke at dawn, then worked on the *Huntress* until the fading light and his aching muscles forced him to rest. It didn't take long for him to move a cot into the carriage house so he could stay close to the hulking Cataphract, saving himself the time and effort of dragging himself back to the main house each evening.

Periodically, he had visitors: Turquo brought food, Lily tried to beg said food off him, and Lady Fenvale (or more rarely, her father) checked on his progress. Victor started seeing time less as a matter of hours and days, and more in a series of interlocking tasks. There were a certain number of bolts to each steel plate, then a certain number of plates to each of the *Huntress'* limbs, and so on. Victor rigged up a clever series of pulleys and winches so he could move the *Huntress'* heavier components by himself, but it was still long, exhausting, satisfying work.

Victor documented his work, sketching the inner workings of the *Huntress* as he broke her down, piece by piece, layer by layer. He recorded every part he removed, refurbished, or replaced, from the smallest rivet to the intricate working of the *Huntress'* motive gears. The deeper Victor went into the Cataphract's mechanisms, the older they got, until he reached the *Huntress'* most ancient component: her alchemical furnace. It was a sphere of rough, grayish-blue stone the size of a small melon, wrapped in a web of metal valves and tubing to connect it to the rest of the Cataphract's mechanisms.

Every other part of the *Huntress*, from the smallest bolt to the intricate motive gears of her joints, had no doubt been replaced at some point or another during her centuries of service. But the alchemical furnace was the ancient and irreplaceable heart of the machine, taken from the Kingsforge and bestowed to the Fenvales by the Crown centuries ago.

Under normal circumstances, only the most experienced members of a Cataphract's crew would ever handle an alchemical furnace. Then again, under normal circumstances, the *Huntress* would have a proper crew, instead of a single alchemical engineer who technically hadn't graduated yet. As Victor ran his fingers over the stone of the *Huntress'* alchemical furnace, he marveled at the opportunity. Even with his university education, it would have been years before he would have been allowed to handle such an important component. He didn't let himself linger, only taking enough time to make sure the alchemical furnace was still in good condition before he secured it back in place.

While Count Fenvale had procured a respectable variety of raw materials, Victor still had to improvise on some key components. He coated the inside of an old stovepipe with heat-resistant ceramic, then used it to replace the *Huntress'* slag-clogged exhaust tubes. A set of old but still serviceable coach springs went into the *Huntress'* ankles, and a couch from Count Fenvale's study provided leather cushions for the helm seat. Per his thesis, Victor integrated the leather bellows from the blacksmith's forge into her air intake; he made sure to triple-check the *Huntress'* structural bolts beforehand. He hammered rivets, strung cables, oiled gears, tightened bolts. Each turn of the wrench was a step closer to making *Huntress* whole again, a step closer to returning her to former glory.

But there was only so much Victor could do.

"My apologies, Lady Fenvale," Victor said as he laid out a large diagram of the *Huntress* on a table between them. The sketches showed the massive Cataphract broken down into pieces, laid out like a vivisectionist's project. "I'm not good enough of a smith to match the fluting of the original plate, so I just focused on making sure the new pauldron fits into place without hindering the *Huntress'* mobility. Which it doesn't, for the record. It won't look so mismatched once I apply some white paint. But I don't have the pigments necessary to match the enameling on the original armor."

"But the armor will hold, yes?" Lady Fenvale looked over Victor's shoulder, up at where the *Huntress* loomed behind him. Even with the mismatched plating, the Cataphract looked far more formidable than she had when Victor started the project. The *Huntress'* visor yawned open like the maw of some strange beast with control levers for teeth and a chair at the back of its throat.

"Well, yes," Victor said.

"Then it'll do. Anything else?" Lady Fenvale returned her attention to Victor's sketches.

"There's also the matter of the *Huntress'* armament. Or lack thereof."

"You're the engineer. Make something."

"If only it were that easy. I don't have the equipment, the materials, or the time to forge a Cataphract-sized weapon from scratch. Even Marissa--er, a fellow student at university, the best smith I've ever met--couldn't produce a proper sword in the short amount of time we've got."

"We're in a forest," Lady Fenvale said. "Find a tree of the correct size, then we'll cut it down and stick a blade at one end. Make a spear. Or a mace."

"That would be ... possible, if not exactly advisable. It's better to treat the lumber first. It's something of a lengthy process, but essential if you don't want the wood to shatter the first time you land a blow. But if you insist, I could probably make something ornamental in time to impress the marquis."

Lady Fenvale frowned. "What are you talking about?"

"That's why you want the *Huntress* operational by the Summer's Steel festival, isn't it? So you can use it to make a grand entrance at the marquis' party?"

"What? No." Lady Fenvale rubbed at the bridge of her nose. "And here I thought you were supposed to be clever."

"I am clever." Victor let the last two weeks' fatigue make him peevish. "Possibly even brilliant. In my field, at least."

"Which obviously isn't politics." Lady Fenvale sighed and shook her head. "The last thing I want to do is take the *Huntress* to my cousin's party. Without an express invitation to do so, bringing a Cataphract to another noble's estate is basically a declaration of war. A war that we couldn't win, even with the *Huntress*."

"Then why do you want her operational by then?"

"Because that is when the marquis will be distracted," Lady Fenvale said. "While my cousin's busy with his party, he'll be far less likely to interfere with the rest of the plan."

"Which is?" Victor asked.

Lady Fenvale leaned on the diagram-laden table for a moment, closed her eyes, and took in a deep breath. "I suppose it's better you know sooner, rather than later."

"Know what, exactly?"

"They teach history at the university, don't they? And law?"

"Well, yes. Though I chose to focus on other subjects." Victor smoothed out a wrinkle in the corner of one of his drawings.

"In that case, have you heard of the Cataphract Oath?"

"In passing. I thought it was a contrivance made up for knight

45

plays?"

"It's real--at least, in that it's still part of kingdom law. It dates back to the first Brethren war, some three hundred years ago. When the Brethren of the Chain captured Kingsforge, King Guy the Fourth suddenly found his army without a way to build new Cataphracts. So he created the Cataphract Oath. Anyone in possession of an operational Cataphract could march their machine before the throne and pledge themselves--and their machine--to the service of the king. In return, they would be awarded with lands and a title ... once the Brethren were conveniently routed, that is. It was a desperate move, but it worked. Most of the ruling families of the kingdom can trace their lineage back to someone who took the Cataphract Oath."

"But you're already a noblewoman," Victor said.

"And that's the problem. Per the Fenvale family charter, women of our line cannot own property, land or otherwise." Her eyes strayed to the *Huntress* once again. "My ancestor was ... short sighted."

"But if you pledge yourself to the throne--"

"I'll be able to establish a new family charter, one that doesn't have me under Maldrinne's thumb. I might not get my father's holding, but I'll still have the *Huntress*. The world looks a lot different from the helm of a Cataphract." Lady Fenvale drew her dark eyes away from the *Huntress* and peered intently at Victor. "An operational Cataphract, that is. She will be operational, yes?"

"Y-yes, of course." Victor shriveled beneath Lady Fenvale's cool, piercing gaze and did a few rough calculations in his head. "In fact, if you're not concerned with the *Huntress'* more cosmetic components, she's theoretically capable of moving under her own power now--"

"She can march?" Lady Fenvale's typically dour expression brightened to one of almost girlish enthusiasm.

"Theoretically?" Victor said. "I wanted to wait until I had everything in place before trying any field tests--"

"We'll test her now," Lady Fenvale said, with all the authority of a royal decree. Before Victor could sputter his protest, Lady Fenvale took to the rickety scaffolding around the *Huntress*. She climbed fearlessly upward, heedless of the way the planks and ladders wobbled with each step. Victor cringed, but Lady Fenvale made it to the *Huntress'* helm. She dropped herself into the helm seat, then surveyed the array of control levers in front of her.

"You didn't rearrange the controls, did you?" Lady Fenvale's voice carried through the carriage house, echoing off the tall ceiling.

"There wasn't any need to--"

"Good!" Lady Fenvale pulled a brass-plated handle, and the machine shuddered to life. Victor envisioned the Cataphract's inner workings as clearly as if they were laid bare before him. The alchemical furnace, the motive gears, the control cables, all working in orchestrated union to bring the *Huntress* to life.

Lady Fenvale laughed, clear and sunny, like a young girl given a pony. She worked the controls with steady ease, and the *Huntress* stood. It was a slow, unsteady movement, at the same time made majestic by the Cataphract's scale. The Cataphract's joints creaked even after the gallons of grease Victor had worked into them over the previous weeks. Boards snapped and clattered to the ground as the *Huntress* pushed past the makeshift scaffolding, like a great beast escaping from a wooden cage. Victor feared the carriage house's thick ceiling beams would break next, but even with the visor open, the *Huntress* had just enough room to stand up straight. Almost as if the carriage house had been built for the purpose, he realized.

The *Huntress* took a slow, lurching step forward, and then another, managing somehow not to crush any of Victor's equipment (or Victor himself) beneath her feet. An enormous arm rose, and the *Huntress* gently placed her open palm on the carriage house's massive doors and pushed them open, letting sunlight stream into the workshop. White-enameled armor reflected the afternoon sun, and suddenly the Cataphract was no longer an intricate engineering project. She was the *Huntress*, a proud, magnificent machine, striding out into the world after too long a slumber. Victor stared at the *Huntress*, mind processing the fact that he was the only reason the damaged, neglected Cataphract could walk again. His awe gave out to more practical matters as he noticed a hitch in the stride of the *Huntress*' right leg. Had he strung the tendon-cables too tight? Or--

Victor paled.

He scrambled to follow the *Huntress* as she marched out into the open air. Count Fenvale rushed out of the manor house, no doubt drawn by the unmistakable, heavy footsteps of an operational Cataphract. Turquo and Lily followed. The former tried to get his master to slow down while the latter just let out a booming, excited bark.

"You did it!" Count Fenvale shouted. Perhaps it was the natural sunlight, but he somehow looked a decade younger as he stared up at the *Huntress*' open visor and the laughing woman at the helm. "Damnation, Diana! You did it!"

Distracted as he was, Victor didn't even protest Lady Fenvale getting the credit for his work. Work that would go to waste if he didn't do something soon. He circled around to the *Huntress*' left, trying to get into Lady Fenvale's line of sight without being crushed beneath the Cataphract's massive feet. He waved his arms over his head and shouted an incoherent, panicked warning, but he couldn't be heard over the din of laughing aristocrats, clanking machinery, and the barking of a very large dog. Victor dashed in front of the *Huntress*, where he could see into the Cataphract's open visor. He waved and yelled some more, but Lady Fenvale ignored him. The *Huntress* saluted Count Fenvale, right gauntlet clenched over the wide breastplate. The celebratory chaos continued for a few minutes longer, until an even louder sound drowned them all out.

Metal ground on metal, like the gnashing of a gargantuan beast's teeth. The snap of shattering steel rang out, and the *Huntress* lurched as her right knee buckled beneath her. Lady Fenvale yanked hard on the control levers, snapping the *Huntress*' arms forward to catch her fall and keep the Cataphract from falling upon her face. Wagon-sized hands plowed deep furrows in the ground, and a teeth-rattling impact roiled through the earth, but at least the *Huntress* didn't take any more damage to go with her ruined knee.

Lady Fenvale locked the *Huntress* into place, undid the belt holding her in the helm seat, and clambered out of the wounded Cataphract. No sooner had she landed on her feet, she lunged forward to grab Victor by the straps of his leather work apron.

"You said she was ready!" Lady Fenvale snarled, and shook Victor for good measure.

"For testing!" Victor yelped. "I said she needed testing! Which, incidentally, you just did. Test the *Huntress*, that is."

"Diana." Count Fenvale limped up behind his daughter and laid a hand on her shoulder. "Enough. It's not his fault."

Lady Fenvale blinked, then slowly let go of Victor. "It's not?"

The count leaned heavily on his cane as he looked over at the felled *Huntress*. "It's the motive gears, isn't it?"

"The right knee's articulator assembly, to be precise." Victor smoothed out his apron, glad to change the subject. "Given the way the *Huntress* was stored in a kneeling position, extra pressure would have been placed on that leg. It's, er, standard procedure, actually, as the crouching position makes it easier to access a Cataphract's inner workings. It's just that leaving the *Huntress* like that for years ... it would be enough to subtly warp the gears--and once that happens, it was only a matter of time before the entire mechanism blew out. I suppose we should be grateful that it happened so soon, and not out on the march," Victor said.

"So every joint in the *Huntress* is going to tear itself apart the next time she moves?" Lady Fenvale said.

"Probably not?" Victor held his hands up placatingly. "The good news is, since all the pressure was on the knee joint, that's probably the only one that got warped."

Lady Fenvale didn't miss a beat. "Then what's the bad news?"

"Er, right. The bad news is that motive gear mechanisms are intricate pieces of machinery, only slightly less advanced than the alchemical furnace itself, meaning--"

"You can't build one from scratch," Lady Fenvale groaned.

"That is correct, yes."

Lady Fenvale rubbed the bridge of her nose between two fingers. "Should I bother asking if we have a spare?"

"I'm afraid we don't, Lady Fenvale. Though, honestly, I wouldn't expect you to have one on hand to begin with. They can be delicate--and therefore prohibitively expensive. Even a full squadron of Cataphracts on the march might only have a handful of spares between them."

"He's right." Count Fenvale spoke up again. "Hell, during the Ducourt Campaign, we didn't even have that. Had to salvage whatever we could off fallen Cataphracts--didn't matter what side they were from. Hell, by the end, the Warden must have had parts from a half dozen Cataphracts bolted on. Or was it the Wellspring?"

"That's the traditional solution, yes," Victor said. "But, ah, we'd need a crippled Cataphract to salvage the motive gears from."

"Not a crippled Cataphract," Lady Fenvale mused. Lily walked up beside her and leaned against her thigh, and the swordswoman rubbed absently at the big dog's ears, thinking. A slow, predatory smile crossed her face. She looked over her shoulder, to where Turquo stood, unflappable as always. "Turquo, how long till the Summer's Steel festival?"

"A week and a day, my lady," Turquo said smoothly.

"Oh. Right. The deadline." Victor winced. "I'm afraid it's going to be impossible to source the proper parts in such a short--"

"You're not going to 'source,' anything, Victor," Lady Fenvale said, and shared a knowing grin with her father. "After all, the marquis is sure to have the *Guilt of Gold* on display for his party."

The pieces clicked into place, and Victor felt his stomach drop for the second time that day. "You can't mean--"

"It's simple. You can't build the part we need." Lady Fenvale rubbed her dog's neck with one hand and set the other on the hilt of her saber. "So we're going to steal one instead."

CHAPTER 7

Upon examination, the damage to the *Huntress* wasn't as severe as Victor had feared: the control cables hadn't snapped, and the furnace piping hadn't ruptured. Assuming they could find replacement parts, the repair would be easy--insomuch as anything related to Cataphract maintenance could be "easy."

While he worked, Lady Fenvale paced in and out of the carriage house like an indecisive cat. She finally stopped once Victor set the damaged motive gear assembly on his workbench, then walked over to peer at the mangled mechanism. The saucer plate–sized motive gears were arranged in parallel formation along a single axle. Several of them were warped and twisted out of shape, with one of the larger (and more important) ones broken entirely in half.

"Are they usually this size?" Lady Fenvale clasped her hands behind her back as she leaned forward to examine the part.

"For a duelist-class Cataphract, yes. A siegebreaker would have larger ones, and a skirmisher smaller, obviously," Victor said.

Lady Fenvale straightened up. "Can I touch it?"

"Er, I suppose so," said Victor. "It's not as if it matters if you break it again--"

"Point." Lady Fenvale took the mechanism in both hands and lifted it experimentally off the table. She let out a soft grunt of effort, but otherwise showed no difficulty in moving the heavy device. She set it back down, then wiped grease from her hands on a mostly clean rag. "The important part is, it's not too big or too heavy to put into a saddlebag."

Lady Fenvale discarded the rag and turned her attention to the *Huntress*. She stepped up onto the wooden crates Victor had set up in front of the Cataphract's right leg and peered into the open cavity. "Once you have a new mechanism, how long will it take you to install it?"

"Several hours. Maybe a day. It depends on how the bolt patterns align, and how the replacement part is calibrated." Victor absentmindedly picked up the dirty rag from where Lady Fenvale had dropped it on the dirt floor.

"Is there anything you can do ahead of time? To make the process faster? The sooner we get the *Huntress* moving, the better off we'll be."

"That ... is an interesting question." Victor rubbed at his chin, then went back to his workbench so he could start paging through his sketched notes and diagrams. "It might be possible to assemble some of the components out of order, so that when the time came, all I'd have to do is install the motive gears and bolt the plating back on--"

"Do it," Lady Fenvale said, and stepped down from her perch. "Once you're done, talk to Turquo. He'll get you properly attired. Maldrinne's staff wouldn't let you into the stables looking like you do now."

Victor looked down at himself. The leather blacksmith's apron had gotten the worst of it, but there was no denying Lady Fenvale's point. "I don't imagine the marquis' staff have been working on a Cataphract nonstop for the last few weeks, either."

Lady Fenvale smiled. "That's what I'm counting on."

"This will do," Turquo said with all the enthusiasm of an obituary.

Victor looked at his outfit in his bedchamber's mirror. Turquo had provided him with striped yellow trousers, a deep blue doublet with brass buttons and pleats around the sleeves, and a broad-brimmed hat of black felt. The clothes were stiffly starched and carried the stale smell of several years inside an old trunk. At least the footwear was comfortable; Turquo had taken the broken-in boots Victor had worn to Fenvale Manor and polished them to an appropriately impressive shine. The whole ensemble had the feel of a uniform, even without any badges of rank anywhere. Victor tugged at the starched-stiff cuffs and rolled his neck, wondering how long it'd take for the outfit to actually become comfortable.

"It's ... nice," Victor said.

"Lady Fenvale instructed that I provide you with one more accessory." Turquo took one of the ubiquitous swords from where it hung on the wall. He took the rapier out of its scabbard to inspect it, nodded his approval, then slid it back into place as he turned back around. Victor sputtered a protest, but Turquo ignored his words with a servant's selective deafness. He draped a leather baldric across Victor's chest, allowing the heavy sword to hang at his left hip.

"There must have been a mistake." Victor braced himself against the sudden, alien weight of the weapon. "I--I don't know how to use a sword."

"But I do," Lady Fenvale said from the doorway.

"In that case, shouldn't you be the one wearing it?" Victor turned around, and his scabbard clattered loudly against the legs of a nearby chair.

"I would if I could," Lady Fenvale huffed. Silk skirts rustled around her ankles as she strode into the room. Victor blinked, realizing this was the first time he'd seen her in a dress. She wore a fawn-brown riding habit of a practical cut, which allowed her to move more freely than Victor's starched attire did. A maroon sash crossed her waist, adding color to the otherwise plain ensemble. Like Victor, she kept the same footwear; the tips of her riding boots poked out from the hem of her skirt. Lady Fenvale still looked annoyed, either from having to wear a skirt, or (more likely) from not wearing a sword.

"But apparently, it's improper for a lady to go about openly armed. Which is why you're going to carry this for me." In a smooth, neat motion, Lady Fenvale grabbed the hilt of the rapier and slid it from its scabbard, testing its weight and balance in her gloved hand.

"Is that necessary?" Victor shied away from the blade and forced a smile. "Perhaps a subtler approach might be better? I mean, if you really, absolutely needed a weapon, which I sincerely hope you won't, why not just bring something small and concealable?"

"Who's to say I haven't?" Lady Fenvale twirled the sword around, then stepped in close to Victor so she could slide it back into the scabbard at his hip. "But sometimes it's better to have a proper sword handy. Just try not to get into any duels if I'm not around."

"Duels?" Victor's voice cracked.

"I expect there will be at least a few," Lady Fenvale said with a shrug. "Get enough 'gentlemen' together, and it won't be long before they start poking holes in each other out of boredom. I wouldn't worry. So long as you don't make an ass of yourself, nobody will bother challenging you. There's no prestige in carving up nobodies."

"I'll keep that in mind." Victor looked down at the sword once more. "But, ah, arms and attire aside, just ... what is the plan, exactly? Surely you don't intend to hold the marquis at swordpoint to take what you need."

"Tempting, but no," Lady Fenvale said with a wry smile. "The Summer's Steel festival is as good a distraction as we could ask for. While the marquis and his guests are busy gossiping and getting stinking drunk, we should have ample opportunity to get what we need and then slip off with the rest of the guests when it's over. The marquis will likely have the *Guilt of Gold* set up for display--meaning he won't move it for awhile. Which means he won't even notice anything is missing until we're gone. Provided you put everything back together how you found it, that is."

"But what about my tools? I haven't even packed anything yet. Not to mention it's far easier to hide a dagger in your boot than it is to traipse around with a full set of torsion wrenches."

"My cousin maintains a full workshop for the *Guilt of Gold* on his estate. You can borrow tools from there," Lady Fenvale said.

Victor groaned. Stealing a vital part was one thing, but using another engineer's tools to do it struck him as downright blasphemous. Per the usual, Lady Fenvale ignored his misgivings and pressed on. "If you have any other questions, we can discuss them while we ride. I've already saddled the horses. Turquo, you've got more clothes packed for Victor, don't you?"

"Of course, my lady." Turquo took a tightly packed valise out of the trunk. "I'll secure your baggage while you bid goodbye to the count."

Count Fenvale waited for them in the main hall, sitting in a high-backed chair, with Lily curled up by his feet. At the sound of footsteps, both of them stood, though Lily sprang up far faster than the count did. Even still, the old man smiled, eyes gleaming.

"Do you have everything you need?" Count Fenvale tottered over to his daughter, then looked her up and down, with both a father's concern and an officer's appraisal. "Provisions? Weapons? Money?"

"Yes, Father," Lady Fenvale said.

"Good." The count nodded, then squinted at Victor. "And you? Are you ready?"

Victor wondered if stern, penetrating gazes were a family trait of the Fenvales. Still, he screwed his expression into what he hoped could pass as bravery. "As much as I can be, my lord."

"You'd better be. You're all she's got," Count Fenvale said. "If I had my way, I'd send a whole damn regiment with you."

"If we could afford to feed a regiment, we wouldn't have to steal the part to begin with," Lady Fenvale noted.

"You should at least take Turquo. There's not a better man to be found in the whole damn kingdom."

"Which is why he needs to stay here." Lady Fenvale's voice was gentle, affectionate. "Someone's got to keep you out of trouble."

"Not much trouble to get into all the way out here," the count grumbled.

"If anyone could find it, it'd be you." Lady Fenvale lowered herself into a crouch so she could ruffle Lily's floppy ears. The dog grunted happily, and curled her tongue out to lick the tip of Lady Fenvale's nose. "And try not to spoil Lily too much while I'm gone, either."

"Couldn't spoil her any more than you do," Count Fenvale said.

Lady Fenvale laughed softly, then stood.

Count Fenvale pulled his daughter into a gentle hug, leaning up to murmur something else into her ear, only to break out into wet coughing. Lady Fenvale immediately eased him back into his chair, and Turquo appeared out of nowhere with a glass of the steaming herbal concoction Victor had suggested days earlier. Count Fenvale gulped down the leafy tea and his breathing eased. Somewhat. Lily whined in concern, while Victor found himself frozen, unsure.

"I'm fine, dammit," Count Fenvale said hoarsely. He waved his daughter and his servant off. "No need for all this fuss. Especially when you've got bigger things to worry about."

"Of course, Father." Lady Fenvale tugged on a pair of riding gloves. "Be well. When we return, you'll see the *Huntress* march again."

Count Fenvale smiled. "I'm looking forward to it."

CHAPTER 8

"Here we are."

Lady Fenvale reined her horse to a halt at the top of the hill, and Victor followed suit. The engineer tilted the brim of his hat to shield his eyes from the early afternoon glare and looked out over Maldrinne Valley. In stark contrast to the muddy forest they'd left behind them days before, Maldrinne Valley was picturesque, its lush green farmland bisected by the white stone of a Cataphract road.

A steady stream of wagons and carriages traveled down that road, all headed for Marquis Maldrinne's sprawling manor at the other end of the valley. If the size of the palatial house wasn't obvious enough, the *Guilt of Gold* stood by the side of the road, her black-and-gold armor polished to a near-blinding sheen. Victor noted the lack of smoke coming from the *Guilt of Gold*'s exhaust vents and wondered how long the Cataphract had been standing there with her furnace unlit.

Banners bearing the *Guilt of Gold*'s coin-and-dagger sigil hung from tall poles planted to either side of the Cataphract, flapping gently in the summer wind. Some of the carriages bore Cataphract sigils as well, painted onto the sides or stitched into flags draped over the back. Victor spotted the crossed spears and twined flowers of the *Rose Lancer*, as well as the snarling lion's head of the *Temper*. Marquis Maldrinne had quite the guest list, Victor realized.

"We'll spend the first few days scouting." Lady Fenvale spoke with all the easy confidence Victor lacked. "That should be enough time to get the lay of the land and locate what we need. Once we do, we can make a more specific plan. Until then, keep your mouth shut and look like you're having a good time."

Victor attempted a smile. "I should be able to manage that. But--"

"But?"

"I've met the marquis before. Only briefly, mind you, some months ago, but he still might recognize me."

"I doubt he will. My cousin is ludicrously rich. Which means he talks to dozens of people every day. He can't be bothered to remember most of them unless they're in a position to make him richer. Which, I presume, you weren't."

"Not exactly, no," Victor admitted.

"Then you've got nothing to worry about. In all likelihood, he's forgotten you already." Lady Fenvale nudged her horse into motion with her heels. "Now come on, let's make an entrance."

They trotted down the hill and joined the train of ornate carriages, keeping a polite distance from the last one in line. One by one, the carriages clattered up to a small pavilion tent set up in the *Guilt of Gold*'s shadow. Men in black-and-yellow livery greeted each arriving baroness or count, offering glass goblets of wine for them to enjoy on the final stretch of their journey. The noblemen and noblewomen laughed and toasted the marquis' generosity before tossing their empty glasses out the windows of their carriages, where they were soon crushed to sparkling dust beneath the next set of hooves and wheels. The baggage wagons split off from their masters, circling around to somewhere behind the marquis' manor while the aristocracy went up to the front door, where they were announced with more bugling and pageantry.

Victor watched the routine repeat itself over and over, soon realizing that he and Lady Fenvale were the only guests without a carriage of their own, much less a second or third wagon to carry their baggage and servants. He fidgeted with his glasses, feeling terribly underdressed even in his borrowed finery.

Despite the mud on her boots and the dust on her skirts, Lady Fenvale carried herself with her typical brazen confidence, though the liveried footmen didn't notice.

"Servants' entrance is around back," one of the servants said, waving them onward.

"Excuse me?" Lady Fenvale glared down at the one who spoke.

"The servants' entrance is in the back," the footman said, exasperated. "I don't care what backwater you're from, but the marquis insists on things being done properly. Only baronets and their betters are allowed to walk in through the front doors. Can't have the rabble tracking mud all over the place."

"Then it's a lucky thing that my father is Count Fenvale," Lady Fenvale said, deadpan. In a quick, sharp motion, she pulled out her invitation as if she were drawing a pistol. Once the footman saw the wax seal pressed into it, he reacted as if she had. Meanwhile, Victor found a new appreciation for Lady Fenvale's icy glare once it was pointed at somebody else.

The footman gawped at the invitation for a moment, then looked up to its bearer--only to cast his eyes downward as he made a deep, apologetic bow. His fellows blinked and followed suit. "My apologies, Lady Fenvale, I didn't know--"

"It's luckier still that my father wasn't able to attend. If you had insulted him like this, he would have challenged you to a duel on the spot." She snapped her fingers, and one of the other servants hurried forward with two goblets of wine, one for Lady Fenvale and the other for Victor. "You're lucky I'm more forgiving than he is."

"Undeservedly lucky, my lady." The footman kept his eyes on the glass-strewn ground. "But please, allow your humble servant to make amends."

"Very well." Lady Fenvale affected a sigh, then waved her hand vaguely at the servant. "Run and tell your master that I have arrived and that I shall make my entrance shortly. Through the front door."

"At once, my lady," The footman sputtered, and then took off at a sprint towards the main house. The rest of the servants hurried to provide refreshments to Victor and Lady Fenvale. She took her time in drinking the refreshing, cool wine, giving the footman plenty of time to announce their arrival. During the wait, Victor looked up at the towering form of the *Guilt of Gold*. Just weeks before, he would have been awed to stand so close to such a famous, magnificent machine. But after working on the *Huntress* for so long, he couldn't help but compare the *Guilt of Gold* to his own work.

The *Guilt of Gold* was far more impressive a sight, Victor admitted to himself. She was taller, broader, and simply shinier than the *Huntress*. The black-armored duelist held her broadsword with the point stuck into the ground and both hands on the pommel in a suitably imperious pose. Impressive as it was, leaving the blade stuck into the dirt struck Victor as an easy way to dull the point of the enormous weapon.

The more Victor studied the *Guilt of Gold*, the more he tallied the hours and hours of work it must have taken to make her black armor shine as it did. And if it rained on the Cataphract while she was still out in the open, the crew would have to start all over again. Victor eyed a passing gray cloud, wary.

As he sized up the machine, Victor realized the *Guilt of Gold*'s pose was off--her stance was too narrow, heels nearly touching. Not that there was anything that could knock a Cataphract over (save for another Cataphract), but to keep the legs locked in such a pose for so long could put unnecessary stress on her joints and motive gears. It'd be far better to let her rest on one knee, or at least with her feet wider apart, but that wouldn't look as impressive, Victor supposed.

"Cheers!" Lady Fenvale finished her drink, then dashed her glass to the ground. The sound of breaking glass snapped Victor out of his thoughtful reverie. Lady Fenvale cleared her throat and rode her horse towards Maldrinne House at an easy walk. About halfway between the Cataphract road and the manor house, Victor leaned in to speak to Lady Fenvale.

"I thought we didn't want to draw attention," he said.

"It's what the servants expect." Lady Fenvale tilted her chin up to a haughty angle. "I might not have a fine carriage or a wardrobe of silken dresses, but haranguing the staff is always in fashion. So long as people see me as a spoiled, eccentric aristocrat who's decided to cause problems for her cousin, they won't realize why I'm really here."

"There's ... something of a logic to that, I admit." Victor pushed his glasses further up his nose. "But where do I fit in? You don't want me to start throwing things at the help now, do you?"

"Officially, you are here in the capacity of my mathematics tutor," Lady Fenvale said. "Which is to say, you're the poor sod my father has tasked with looking after me while I make an ass of myself."

"I'm supposed to be your chaperone?" Victor blinked.

"I never said you were supposed to be good at it," Lady Fenvale noted. "All you'll have to do is stay close and look vaguely scandalized."

"You make it sound so easy," Victor said, deadpan.

"Getting into character already. Good." Lady Fenvale nodded in approval, then spurred her horse onward.

By the time Victor and Lady Fenvale made it to the manor house proper, a small crowd of obsequious servants and curious nobles had gathered to greet them. Lady Fenvale's skirts fluttered about her boots even as she dismounted with the ease of a cavalry officer. Victor followed, albeit with far less grace. His knees and thighs ached from the last several days' riding, but he kept himself from falling over, at least.

"My dear cousin!" a booming voice said. The guests and servants parted, revealing Marquis Maldrinne, dressed in sable black and gold braid. His short cape fluttered behind him as he descended the steps to bow politely to Lady Fenvale. "I was under the impression you wouldn't be attending."

"Circumstances changed," Lady Fenvale said with a casual shrug. "My father sends his regards."

"How is the old campaigner, anyway?" Marquis Maldrinne straightened and offered his left elbow to Lady Fenvale. He spoke louder than strictly necessary, performing for the rest of his guests. A few of the more curious guests sized Victor up, but Lady Fenvale and the marquis kept most of their attention.

"Better than ever." Lady Fenvale linked arms with the marquis and faked a sunny smile. Seeing the marquis in his finery and Lady Fenvale in her dusty travel garb made Victor think back to the *Guilt of Gold* and the *Huntress* once again.

"Is that so?" Marquis Maldrinne said. "That's certainly good to hear. My messenger informed me the good count was unable to receive my invitation personally. He gave me the impression that my dear uncle was laid up in bed."

"Quite the opposite, actually. My father happened to be out riding at the time. He likes the exercise," said Lady Fenvale.

"As do you, apparently." Marquis Maldrinne glanced over his shoulder, looking past Victor to where the stable boys led the horses off. "It's a long ride from here to Fenvale Manor."

"For some, perhaps." Lady Fenvale patted the marquis on the arm. "But I prefer to travel light."

"I can see that," Marquis Maldrinne said. "I'm surprised you didn't bring that dog of yours."

"Lily doesn't like crowds."

"Pity." Marquis Maldrinne looked back, finally noting Victor's existence. "But it appears you've taken in another stray, nonetheless?"

"Mm?" Lady Fenvale arched a brow, curious, and then finally realized. "You mean Victor? I suppose that's one way to describe him. I've recently taken an interest in the sciences, and my father thought I should have a formal tutor."

"Victor Brinden, at your service, my lord.." Victor bowed and doffed his hat, polite.

"He's a bit ... awkward, but quite clever." Lady Fenvale spoke about Victor as if he wasn't even there. "University educated, you know."

"Is he, now?" The marquis turned around to regard Victor carefully. Victor swallowed, mouth suddenly dry despite the wine he'd had mere minutes earlier. Would Marquis Maldrinne remember him from his disastrous presentation, months ago? Or would Victor's finer clothes be enough of a disguise? Victor hoped the marquis wouldn't recognize him so long as nothing exploded.

"You seem fairly young for a full master, Victor," Marquis Maldrinne said.

"I--I'm still technically a journeyman, sir." Victor stammered out a nervous reply. "I'm just pursuing some other projects until I can finalize my studies. Count Fenvale has been generous enough to employ me in the meanwhile.."

"I'll have to introduce you to my staff--I only let the best engineers in all Leovaix work on my Cataphract." Marquis Maldrinne proudly looked in the direction of the *Guilt of Gold*, standing tall a half mile away. "Perhaps they might even teach you something."

"I'll look forward to it, sir," Victor said.

"Good!" Marquis Maldrinne clapped Victor on the shoulder hard enough to stagger him, then turned on one heel. "But that can wait. You two must be parched after such a long journey. Let's get you something to drink, hm? While we're at it, I can make a few introductions. I'm afraid your friend Lady Rosalind was unable to make it, Cousin, but surely we can find somebody who'll bother speaking with you."

The marquis led them through the main doors into Maldrinne House's main hall. The room stretched up three full stories, tall enough to house a Cataphract. Not that Victor would ever work in such a finely decorated place, he mused. The floor was tiled in black marble, with matching dark pillars along the sides. Gold inlay wrapped around the pillars in stylized vine patterns, reflecting the light that streamed down from the circular window set in the ceiling. Balconies ringed the second and third stories.

Between all the dark stone and the round window above, Victor got the feeling he'd been tossed into some enormous cauldron, like something out of a children's witch story. And if the room was a cauldron, then the potion it brewed was an expensive one. Silk, lace, and jewels were on flagrant display--and these were just the nobles' traveling clothes, Victor realized. Even some of the Marquis' staff were dressed better than Victor was. Which, admittedly, wasn't a high bar to set. Said servants circled the main hall, doling out puffy pastries and more fine wines. At least this time, nobody smashed their empty glasses on the floor.

Marquis Maldrinne took Lady Fenvale around the room in a slow circuit of introductions, starting with a man with the *Temper*'s lion-head sigil on his doublet and a red-haired woman in dress with a scandalously low-cut neckline.

Victor moved to follow, but Lady Fenvale subtly waved him off. Relieved, Victor retreated to the edge of the room. There, Victor acquired himself a drink from a passing servant and relaxed, however slightly. It had been a close call, but if the Marquis didn't recognize him from the university, that meant no one else would. After all, Lady Fenvale was right. Victor was a nobody. Anyone important enough to warrant an invitation to the Marquis' celebration wouldn't know, or care, about a lowly university student. Victor found the anonymity oddly comforting, like a dark cloak that allowed him to fade into the background while Lady Fenvale went about her scheme.

This lasted for all of three minutes.

"Victor?" came a woman's voice. "Victor Brinden? Is that really you?"

CHAPTER 9

Victor managed not to choke on his drink.

Barely.

She was one of the most beautiful women Victor had ever seen, which made him wonder why she was talking to him in the first place. While not dressed as lavishly as the other guests, that somehow made her all the more stunning, as she didn't need to rely on jeweled baubles and lacy frills to be noticed. Her silken gown was comparatively plain, but it clung to the abundant curve of her figure in an entirely too distracting manner. The woman's one concession to courtly fashion was the complicated-looking coiffure that held her golden curls in check. Even piled up as it was, the top of the woman's hairstyle only came up to the level of Victor's nose, so she had to look up at him with a bemused expression on her lovely, round-cheeked face.

Victor almost didn't recognize her without her forge gloves on.

"Marissa?" Victor asked.

"That's Master Smith Marissa Chalment to you." Marissa winked, then dipped into a playful curtsy.

"My apologies, Master Chalment." Victor found himself smiling the most genuine smile he'd had since he'd left Fenvale Manor. "I shouldn't have forgotten, especially since your graduation party left me hungover for a week. But that was two years ago--what are you doing here?"

"Working on the *Guilt of Gold*, of course," Marissa said, smug. "The finest Cataphract in Leovaix needs the finest crew to work on her."

"Ah. Congratulations," Victor said.

"Thank you, thank you. Though it's not quite as glamorous as it sounds. I've done nothing but polish armor and tighten cables for the last six weeks." She heaved a wistful sigh. "A month or two ago, the marquis said he was going to recruit somebody from the university to help me, but that fell through. Something about an explosion, he said, but the man has a habit of hyperbole."

"Ah. Right. Surely exaggerated." Victor took a sip of his wine.

"But what about you? What are you doing here?" Marissa took in Victor's borrowed finery and the rapier hanging at his hip. She reached forward with one green-gloved hand and flicked the pommel of the weapon. "And since when do you carry a sword?"

"I understand it's the latest fashion," Victor said.

"Unfortunately, it is." Marissa sighed. "Just be careful, will you? Too many so-called gentlemen are far too eager to carve each other up at any excuse."

"Matters of honor are hardly an 'excuse,' my dear lady," a familiar, smooth voice chimed in from somewhere behind Victor.

Victor didn't spill his drink but tightened his fingers around the stem of his wineglass as he turned to face no less than Rochen Dunsall. The big man wore a black cavalryman's tunic, complete with gold buttons, leather riding gloves thrust into his belt, and a basket-hilted sword hanging at his side. White gauze peeked out from his right sleeve, showing he still hadn't recovered from (and certainly not forgotten) their first encounter. "Wouldn't you agree, Journeyman Brinden?"

Marissa's blue eyes flicked between Victor and Dunsall. "Have you two met?"

"In passing," Victor said.

"Not all that long ago, honestly," Dunsall mused. "Though our mutual friend was hardly as well dressed at the time. Or equipped, for that matter. Good to see your fortunes have changed, Brinden."

Victor blinked, unable to think of a proper reply beyond: "Thank you?"

"Honestly, friend--you're turning out to be a remarkable man. First, you turn up in the Fenvales' orbit, and now you apparently are already acquainted with one of the loveliest women I've ever met." Dunsall turned his smile on Marissa, who giggled in reply.

"Flatterer." She patted him fondly on his non-bandaged arm. Between the swordsman's height and Marissa's lack thereof, she had to pull on his sleeve and stand up on tiptoe in order to plant a playful kiss on his bearded cheek. "Do go on."

Dunsall basked in the attention. "I could. At length. But I don't think you have several hours to spare, and that still wouldn't answer my question."

"If you must know, Victor and I studied at university together. Even though I was a few years ahead of him--I won't tell you how many-- we both apprenticed for Professor Dorrett."

"He, ah, always spoke highly of you," Victor added. "Professor Dorrett, that is."

"I should hope so," Marissa said, smug.

"Well then!" Dunsall grinned wolfishly at Victor. "I'll look forward to seeing what else you've got in store."

Victor opened his mouth to protest, to plead his unremarkability, but was interrupted by Marquis Maldrinne's booming voice.

"Attention, everyone!" The marquis had climbed to the hall's second-story balcony so he could be seen as he addressed his guests. His voice echoed from the gleaming marble of his hall. "Now that my cousin has made her unexpected--but by no means unwelcome--arrival, that should be everyone I've invited! Which means that we can get the Summer's Steel festival officially underway!"

A not-entirely-sober cheer rose up through the hall, and the Marquis' guests all raised their glasses in salute. He waited for the applause to die down, then resumed his speech.

"Let me thank each and every one of you for attending! I cannot describe how much pleasure it gives me to see you all today. Every year, we gather to celebrate how our ancestors pushed back against the monstrosities that plagued humanity and thus brought an end to the Behemoth Age.

"I've spared no expense to ensure this festival is worthy of those great heroes--and worthy of you, their descendants, the shining gems of Leovaix's nobility. There shall be music, dancing, drinking, feasting, hunting. Any and every pleasure I have to offer will be at your disposal. In fact, this very evening, I shall present to you a spectacle the likes of which has never been seen before! There are a few last-minute preparations I must attend to. In the meanwhile, my staff will show you to your chambers, so that you may get settled in. Relax and prepare yourselves, my friends, for tonight, you shall be amazed!"

Marquis Maldrinne swept his cape dramatically as he turned to disappear into a hallway branching off from the balcony. Another round of hoisted glasses and cheers echoed through the round hall.

"And that's my cue," Marissa said. "If you'll excuse me, gentlemen--I've work to do."

Victor furrowed his brow. "The marquis needs an alchemical engineer for his party? What for?"

"You'll see." Marissa winked, then dipped into a polite curtsy before leaving.

Once the blonde master smith was out of sight, Victor found himself alone with Dunsall. The swordsman turned his head, watching Marissa leave for a long, lingering moment before he returned his attention to Victor. "It seems she likes you."

"We, ah, were acquainted at the university, yes." Victor retreated a step, only to clatter the tip of his rapier on the marble pillar behind him.

"In that case, let me offer you some advice, friend." Dunsall stepped in close, lowering his voice so only Victor could hear. "I don't know what Lady Fenvale's got planned or why she's dragged a nobody like you into it. What I do know is that it would be in your best interest not to get involved in the affairs of your betters."

"I--I have no idea what you're talking about," Victor said.

"Mmm. All that time at university, and you're still a fool. Tsk." Dunsall affected the tone of an imperious, disappointed schoolmaster with a disturbing amount of accuracy. "You won't get a second warning, friend. Because if you're not careful, you might find yourself having to use that sword you're wearing. Some men will take any excuse to throw a glove in your face."

Dunsall stretched his riding gloves tight between his hands, and Victor swallowed nervously.

"Feel free to tell Lady Fenvale we spoke. Perhaps it'll convince her to stop trying to ruin the marquis' celebration. Not that she can--all she's likely to do is make an ass of herself. Which would be entertaining, but I'd rather not have to clean up afterward. So please, friend, be sensible. It'll make my life easier. Yours too. Now, if you'll excuse me, I have a master smith to charm." Dunsall tapped the brim of his hat with two fingers in a

66

mocking salute, then turned around to step back into the flow of the party.

Hands shaking, Victor looked for another drink.

"We're doomed."

A valet had shown Victor and Lady Fenvale to the guest suite they'd be staying in for the duration of the Summer's Steel festival. Once the door closed, Lady Fenvale wasted little time in checking behind each painting and curtain, searching for peepholes or listening vents. She even went so far as to poke at the walls and floorboards with the tip of a thin stiletto she pulled out of a concealed scabbard in her sleeve. Finally, after her third trip around the room, she deemed it safe for Victor to speak, at which point he filled her in on his conversation with Marissa and Dunsall. At length.

"Absolutely doomed," Victor concluded and rubbed his face with his hands.

"We are not," Lady Fenvale said, and pointedly slid her dagger back into its sheath.

"But Dunsall's already suspicious--which means he's going to tell the marquis."

"Tell him what?" Lady Fenvale asked. "There's nothing Dunsall can tell the marquis he doesn't already know. Except for your history with one of his junior engineers. As for the rest, my cousin knows exactly what he's doing. He sent that invitation out of spite, and I have accepted it in the same manner. And now he's making it a point to insult me as politely as he can. Did you notice how this suite's at the far end of the wing, barely a step above the servants' quarters?"

Victor looked up and glanced around the well-furnished room. Considering he'd spent the last several weeks sleeping in a glorified barn, in the shadow of the *Huntress*, the little suite of rooms was positively decadent. "It is?"

"The window is facing the rear gardens instead of the front, so we can't see who's coming or going. The rooms are far too small--if we'd brought a whole carriage worth of baggage, we wouldn't have enough room to stand. There isn't even a fireplace. These rooms have got to be glacial in

67

the winter. I've seen duels fought over less. Lucky for us, my cousin's 'hospitality' serves our purposes. We're far from the other guests, from the staff, from the festivities in general. Something to keep us out of the way, to keep me from making too much of a commotion. Don't you see? My cousin only expects me to cause some sort of scandal so as to ruin his festival and make him look bad."

"Which is exactly what you have in mind."

"Only as a happy side effect." Lady Fenvale smiled, predatory.

Victor groaned. "How convenient."

"Honestly, I'm beginning to think that this may be too easy. Especially if you can convince your friend the master smith to let you into her workshop." Lady Fenvale paused, then added, "Don't take that as a euphemism."

"A euphemism for--?" Victor started sputtering as soon as the realization hit him. "Lady Fenvale! Are you suggesting that I--I mean, we-- which is to say, Marissa--er, Master Smith Chalment and I--"

Lady Fenvale silenced Victor with a simple hand gesture. "As I said, that wasn't a euphemism. Though the fops and gossips would be happy to take it as such. Which, again, could be in our favor. So long as they're talking about who you may or may not be dallying with, they won't suspect why we're really here."

"How fortunate." Victor took a moment to let the implication set in, and glanced at the door. "They, ah ... they're not going to have that sort of conversation about us, are they?"

Lady Fenvale canted her head to the side and blinked. "Why would they? You haven't been telling them that, have you?"

"Of course not!" Victor's words built momentum as they flowed out of his mouth as fast as politeness allowed. "It's just that, well, you're a young lady, and I'm a young man, and we're in somewhat close quarters, as you've mentioned, so one might make ... presumptions. I mean, I wouldn't. But if someone were so inclined, as you mentioned before--"

"Victor," Lady Fenvale said flatly.

"Yes?"

"Stop talking."

"Thank you." Victor clamped his mouth shut.

"No one is going to make any assumptions about us." Lady Fenvale stood straighter and tilted her chin up to an appropriately condescending angle. "I am, after all, a count's daughter, the scion of a long and noble lineage. You, on the other hand, are not. Moreover, while you are undeniably skilled at your trade, you're certainly not handsome enough or charming enough to make a lady of my standing look past the gap in our respective social stations."

"I'm not sure if I should be relieved or insulted," Victor said.

"What you should be is focused on the things you're actually good at. Trust me, Victor. There's absolutely no chance anyone who knows me-- or anything about me--will think that the two of us are involved. You're quite simply not my type. I've given the gossips enough to yammer on about for a week by just showing up. You just worry about getting your friend to show you her tools." Lady Fenvale frowned. Sighed. "Again, not a euphemism."

"Noted," Victor said. "But you do realize I can't steal a full set of wrenches out from under her nose? Marissa, er, Master Smith Chalment is smarter than that."

Lady Fenvale rolled her eyes. "I didn't tell you to steal anything. Not right away. You can use the first visit to survey the place so you can figure out how to get what you need later."

"You have put a disturbing amount of thought into this, Lady Fenvale."

"It's basic military strategy. Forward reconnaissance can sometimes win a battle before it's even fought."

Victor looked down at the rapier still hanging from his side like a long metal tumor. "You're not going to charge in there and start stabbing people, are you?"

"Of course not. I have a plan." Lady Fenvale crossed her arms over her chest. "Or at least the foundations of one. I'll be able to make more concrete plans once I know how your friend has her parts laid out." She paused, then made it a point to correct herself. "Not a--"

"--euphemism, I know," Victor said.

"Now, if you're done moping about, I need to put on something halfway appropriate for the evening's entertainment." Lady Fenvale shook another puff of road dust out of her riding skirts. "I don't know what kind of spectacle my cousin has planned, but whatever it is, it's going to be big. They've already roped off the whole of the rear gardens for it, and the staff are running themselves ragged in preparation. If the Marquis put half as much effort into his military career as he did into this festival, we'd never have to worry about the Brethren again."

"If he did that, I doubt we'd be able to get away with everything you have planned," Victor said.

"Good point."

CHAPTER 10

That evening, the marquis' guests and their entourages gathered in the gardens behind his sprawling manor house. The groundskeepers had constructed a wooden stage between the trimmed hedges, with a semicircle of chairs and tables facing it. One table, draped with a tablecloth with the *Guilt of Gold*'s dagger-and-coin sigil sewn into it, stood above the others on a three-foot platform, obviously the Marquis' personal seat.

A footman guided Lady Fenvale to a seat at this very table. She had swapped her riding habit for a gown in deep, ruddy red, finely tailored but not nearly as ostentatious as the glittering outfits worn by the rest of the audience. She kept her expression neutral as she sat on the platform, in full view of the rest of the Marquis' guests.

A different footman showed Victor to his own place in a far less visible seat, off to one side and on ground level. There, Victor settled in between a countess' lady-in-waiting and a baronet's horse master, conveniently out of the way. Once all the assigned seats had been filled (save for the empty seat next to Lady Fenvale), servants brought out dinner, course by course.

The enticing scent of the marquis' cuisine reminded Victor he hadn't eaten since that morning, and so he dug into the decadent food with gusto. The savory delicacies melted on his tongue, and by the time Victor finished one exotic dish, the waiters brought over the next. There were partridges stewed in wine and vegetable broth; flaky-crusted meat pies, stuffed with venison and mushrooms; and a whole wild boar, drenched in imported spices, slow-roasted, and ceremoniously portioned out, with the choicest bits going to the marquis' most honored guests. Victor was content to just get a thick slice from one of the back legs.

A troupe of acrobats tumbled onto the stage and launched into their clowning. The seated nobles hooted in laughter and threw their gnawed-upon bones at any performer who missed a step. The marquis had still not yet appeared, leaving Lady Fenvale to dine alone. She appeared to enjoy the food, even if she didn't throw anything.

By the time the servants brought out dessert (candied almonds and delicate flowers sculpted from dried fruit), the acrobats retreated. As they did, a quartet of burly stagehands pushed a set of tall panels into place behind the stage. Made from canvas stretched over wood frames, the panels showed an image of a city street, the stone buildings and cobbled road painted in such a manner as to give the illusion of depth. Once the scenery was in place, a short and portly man walked onto the stage.

"So it's true!" The woman sitting at Victor's left wiped sugar residue from her fingers with a silk napkin. "I'd heard the marquis commissioned Carondel to write him a play, but I didn't think he'd come out personally."

"Must've paid him extra," the horse master at Victor's right muttered through his droopy mustaches.

"Honored guests!" Carondel's voice carried surprisingly well for such a small man. "On behalf of my patron, the great Marquis Maldrinne, I would like to congratulate you! As you, dear gentles, are about to view the first performance of my newest, greatest play! My esteemed patron, a man of impeccable tastes, bid me to write an entertainment, the likes of which has never been seen before. And so, my players and I have labored for weeks, practicing day and night to fulfill this request. Tonight, you lucky few shall watch the first of three plays I have written for this Summer's Steel festival! These historical plays are all part of a greater sequence, specifically written to educate and entertain, and meant to be enjoyed on consecutive evenings. Thusly, I am proud to present to you the first part of this masterwork: A Hero's Arrival!"

Carondel bowed to the polite applause of the audience and slipped off to the side. Once he was out of the way, an actress walked onto the other side of the stage and struck a wide-legged, mock-heroic pose.

She wore a man's boots, trousers, and tunic, all comically oversized, hanging off her body in a manner both ridiculous and suggestive. The neckline of the billowing brown tunic plunged scandalously deep, nearly to her navel, only held in check by thin leather lacing. A thick belt held her pants around her waist, and she wore a sword on her hip long enough to drag across the ground behind her. Her other accessory was a trembling fluff of a dog that she cradled in the crook of her arm, where it growled at anyone and anything it could focus its bulging, panicked eyes on. The dog's constant, choleric barking was loud enough that the actress carrying it had to nearly yell to be heard.

"Come, Father, we must hurry!

"The hour grows late; our friends shall worry!"

The actress looked behind her, and a hunched-over old man followed, leaning heavily on a cane. Despite his comically decrepit age, he wore a full suit of rusted armor, which rattled like a sack full of cookware each time he took a step. The clattering of his armor only agitated the dog further, at which point the panicked puffball's yapping went up an octave. The armored actor ignored it and spoke in a shrill, caricatured tone as he delivered his own lines.

"Yes, yes, my stride is slow.

"But I was faster, long ago.

"My legs were spry, my back was straight.

"For it was I who held the gate,

"'Gainst foes and monsters, beasts and men.

"How I long to live those days again.

"But now I'm old, and I grow weak.

"So now my last quest is to seek

"A worthy heir, to take my place,

"Brave and strong enough to face

"Beast gods, titans, and dragons too.

"To protect this city--and also you."

The actress pouted, then hitched up her voluminous trousers, indignant. Tittering laughter rippled through the audience, and the actress waited for it to die down before she started to speak (again, over the sound of her dog's barking).

"But, Father, can you not see?

"I need no man to protect me.

"Can I not fence? Can I not ride?

"Is this not a longsword at my side?

"'Tis I should be your heir so crown'd!

"Then I'll set out, with loyal hound

"And charging steed, and naked blade.

"Thus shall the Renvallis legend be made!"

"Alice Renvallis" drew her sword and held it aloft. Between the trembling dog and the actress' oversized costuming, she looked like a child pretending at importance, rather than an inspirational figure. The audience laughed harder--which was when Victor realized half the audience wasn't looking at the stage. Instead, they focused their attention somewhere else: on Lady Fenvale.

Even at a distance, Victor could see her pained, too-wide smile. The dog, the sword, the men's clothing--had Marquis Maldrinne commissioned an entire play for the sole purpose of mocking his cousin? The seat next to Lady Fenvale remained empty--though perhaps for the best, as Victor wouldn't have put it past Lady Fenvale to gut the man with her dining knife, if he'd been within arm's reach.

The play went on.

The plot was a flimsy thing, conveyed in Carondel's doggerel verse. The old man was supposed to be Knight-Colonel Renvallis, a name Victor vaguely recalled from one of his history classes at the university. With the Behemoth Age coming to a close, the knight-colonel wanted to retire, but his honor wouldn't let him do so until he found a worthy successor to guard the city of Braveharbor. Meanwhile, his daughter Alice (a name Victor didn't recall ever being mentioned in any histories) wanted nothing more than to be that successor.

Over the course of the first act, the two of them met with a succession of stock characters, each encounter heaping comic humiliation upon Alice. A greedy silk trader cheated Alice out of her money (what little she had). A lusty widow mistook her for a very pretty boy (one of the play's more fantastical fabrications, given Alice's costuming) and flirted outrageously. A clever servant ran verbal and literal circles around her, keeping up a quick-tongued patter of puns, insults, and innuendos for several minutes without stopping to breathe. Even the tiny, nervous dog in the actress' arms got in on the slapstick when it relieved itself on her shirt, though Victor wasn't sure if that was in the script or not.

Each indignity heaped onto Alice earned two waves of laughter:

the first from the bawdy comedy playing out on stage, and the second as the audience turned to watch Lady Fenvale's red-faced reaction. Seated at the center of the audience, surrounded by laughing, mocking faces, Lady Fenvale was trapped. There was no way for her to escape without pushing her way past a half dozen of the other guests.

Between bouts of comic business, the other characters lauded someone called the Errant Knight, praising the unseen man's strength and bravery in the most flowery couplets Carondel could devise. Finally, as the comic japery grew increasingly more convoluted and frantic, a messenger rushed in from stage right, panting.

"Hark! Hark! And hear me well!

"For I have great news to tell.

"From city walls, I did sight--

"The coming of the Errant Knight!"

Stillness took the stage. The messenger cleared his throat, then repeated his line, only louder.

"THE COMING OF THE ERRANT KNIGHT."

There was another moment's stillness--and then the ground shook, hard enough to rattle the plates and cutlery on the feasting tables. The tremor boomed again, then again, in the unmistakable footfalls of a multiton war machine. The footsteps grew louder, closer--and the audience gasped as the *Guilt of Gold* marched into view. Waning sunlight gleamed from her polished armor, giving the black and gold Cataphract an almost divine semblance.

The *Guilt of Gold* marched around the side of Maldrinne House and came to a stop behind the stage. The sheer size of the *Guilt of Gold* dwarfed the actors, reducing them to insignificant insects in comparison to the enormous machine. On cue, fireworks were lit somewhere deeper in the garden, and rockets whizzed up into the air and burst into golden sparks, adding to the spectacle. That the actors held their places was impressive in its own right; Victor knew it took no small degree of courage to stand still so close to moving Cataphract.

The *Guilt of Gold* planted the point of her broadsword into the ground behind the stage, then eased into a kneeling position. The Cataphract's visor levered open, revealing Marquis Maldrinne at her controls. With a toothy, smug grin, he stood up and put one booted foot on the edge of the open visor hatch, striking an ostensibly heroic pose. Below, the actors raised their voices and called out in unison.

"Huzzah! We cheer!

"The Errant Knight is here!"

Marquis Maldrinne bowed to the impressed applause of his guests. This done, he tossed a coil of rope out of the *Guilt of Gold*'s cockpit. With one end anchored somewhere beneath the helm-seat, Marquis Maldrinne used the dangling line to lower himself to the stage, to the affected awe of the assembled cast. The Marquis stumbled a step as his boots set down on the stage's planks, but he soon stepped forward and sketched out another bow to the audience, who replied with a fresh wave of applause.

This done, the Marquis sauntered down from the stage--and up into the audience. He wove his way past the other guests, finally coming to sit down in the empty chair beside Lady Fenvale. He poured himself a glass of wine, then waited for the laughter and commotion to settle down before he spoke.

"Enjoying the play, Cousin?"

CHAPTER 11

"I'm going to kill him." Lady Fenvale paced back and forth with all the frustrated energy of a caged tiger.

That Lady Fenvale had made it through the rest of the performance without stabbing anyone was a testament to her self-control. After Marquis Maldrinne's dramatic arrival, the rest of the play had been devoted to singing the praises of the Errant Knight, culminating in Knight-Colonel Renvallis declaring him his successor (without actually mentioning his name). Once the actors made their bows to the audience's applause, Lady Fenvale had retreated from the gathering as fast as she could manage and barricaded herself in her bedroom until morning.

Victor had thought a night's sleep would have soothed Lady Fenvale's temper, but as soon as he heard her booted footsteps echoing through the small suite, he knew he was wrong. And so, he sat helplessly at the table in the common room and watched Lady Fenvale's fury simmer. The staff had delivered a platter of fruits and cheeses for their breakfast, but neither Victor nor Lady Fenvale had touched it.

"The marquis, or the playwright?" Victor asked.

Lady Fenvale stopped her pacing for a moment to think. A wicked smile crossed her features. "I'm going to kill both of them."

"That's a very funny joke, Lady Fenvale. You are joking, yes?" Victor's eyes flitted towards his sheathed rapier, hanging from a hook on the wall. Thankfully, Lady Fenvale hadn't seized the weapon. Yet. "Er, perhaps you should remember why we came here in the first place?"

"You're right." Lady Fenvale breathed in deeply to steady herself, then ran her hands through her dark hair, composing herself. Some of the tension drained from her shoulders, but not all of it. "Thank you, Victor."

"You're welcome?" Victor said, unsure of what else to say. He hadn't expected Lady Fenvale to actually listen to him. "But, ah ... I do have some good news, at least."

"You do?"

"My friend Marissa--er, that is, Master Smith Chalment--sent me a

77

note." He held up the envelope that had arrived with their breakfast. "It's an open invitation to tour the *Guilt of Gold*'s workshop. So, ah, that's one step closer. Reconnaissance, as you put it?"

"At least something's gone right." Lady Fenvale crossed the room to lean against the windowsill. She stared out over the gardens and the stage set up in them. The *Guilt of Gold* still knelt behind the stage, powered down, but gleaming in the morning sun. "Except--"

"--for the fact that the *Guilt of Gold* is sitting in the middle of the gardens where everyone can see her?" Victor finished Lady Fenvale's sentence. "Not to mention the fact that he's likely to parade her around at some point as part of the play. Even if I bolt the armor plating back on once I've removed the motive gears, the marquis is bound to notice something wrong as soon as he's at the helm."

"I didn't expect my cousin would stoop so low as to use his Cataphract as a ... as a prop." Lady Fenvale seethed. "If he intends to march the *Guilt of Gold* around every night to show her off, that means we have a far smaller window of time to steal the parts you need."

"That is an added obstacle, yes," Victor said.

Lady Fenvale turned away from the window and started pacing again. "I don't know what's worse--that my cousin's parading his Cataphract around like a prize pony, or that he commissioned the most famous playwright in the kingdom to write a play for the sole purpose of mocking me. And it wasn't even a good play, either! I've seen better verse written on a back-alley wall."

"Hold on." Victor turned the facts around in his head with a similar feeling as when he examined gears and bolts to determine the best way to fit them together. "Apart from the somewhat ... pointed nature of the play, it wasn't nearly as good as Carondel's reputation would suggest. The characters were flat stereotypes, the rhyme and meter were uninspired, and the plot was a loosely connected sequence of stock comedy bits that any group of strolling players would already know."

"So he's a hack." Lady Fenvale slowed her pacing enough to pluck a small orange from the breakfast tray and started cutting it up with a knife far larger than the task required.

Victor declined to ask where Lady Fenvale had got the knife from and focused on his reasoning instead. "That may be true. But think. The marquis didn't expect you to actually attend. He only sent his invitation to mock you, as you've said multiple times."

"Indeed."

"Furthermore, one can presume that a play specifically written to mock you wouldn't be as, ah, sadistically satisfying if you weren't there to suffer through it. So what if, when Marquis Maldrinne saw you actually had taken up his invitation, he told Carondel to make some last-minute changes to the play? That certainly might explain the flimsy plot and contrived comedy."

"You may be on to something, Victor." Lady Fenvale popped an orange slice into her mouth and chewed for a few thoughtful moments before returning her attention to the alchemical engineer. "You've brought ink and paper with you, yes?"

"Of course." Victor ducked into his small bedroom and took the requested writing materials out of his valise. "What exactly do you have in mind?"

"My cousin has changed his play at least once." Lady Fenvale took the writing supplies from Victor, then laid them out on a small desk in the corner. She smoothed out a sheet of blank paper, then uncorked the inkpot. "Which means it shouldn't be hard to change it again."

"That's ... feasible." Victor rubbed at his chin. "Fitting, even. But we don't have the kind of money we'd need to commission a play at the last minute. Even if we did, Carondel won't do anything to slander his patron."

"Which is why I'm not going to ask him to." Lady Fenvale picked up a brass-tipped pen and dipped its nib into the inkpot. "You go see about getting that workshop tour while I work on this."

"Of course, Lady Fenvale." Victor nodded. "But, ah ... try not to kill anyone while I'm away?"

"Don't worry about that, Victor." Lady Fenvale's white teeth shone in a predator's smile. "Thanks to you, I've got a better idea."

By mid-morning, Maldrinne House bustled with activity, as the marquis' guests set about their intrigues and amusements while the staff bustled around them, somehow both omnipresent and invisible. The hallways and salons of the house soon grew crowded with hungover aristocrats, slowing Victor down considerably as he tried to pass. Finally, Victor managed to slip out through one of the back doors, across the garden-turned-theater, and to the Cataphract workshop.

The workshop was far bigger and more impressive than the term suggested. It was built from great blocks of limestone, tall enough to house a standing Cataphract. A great arch stretched over the three-story-high doors, with the coin-and-dagger sigil of the *Guilt of Gold* carved into the keystone, in case one forgot which Cataphract was maintained here. The huge main doors hung open, letting light and fresh air inside. The building was about three-quarters of a mile from the main house, tucked away behind a small hill so as to spare Marquis Maldrinne from the sight of anyone performing actual work.

Where Victor had stumbled his way through the manor house with its indolent guests and bustling staff, he felt instantly at place in the busy workshop. If nothing else, he intuitively understood the kind of work being done--and how to stay out of the way. Victor stood at the edge of the massive doorway and watched the crew's efficient routine with no small degree of jealousy. If he'd just thought to use thicker bolts in his experiment--Victor shook his head free of the thought. There was no helping it now.

All through the workshop, young men and women went about the dozens of tasks needed to keep a Cataphract workshop operational. They stoked the forge in the corner, oiled the hoists and pulleys hanging from the ceiling, polished tools, or hauled crates of supplies from one place to another.

In contrast to the ramshackle, improvised tools and scaffolding he had used to work on the *Huntress*, everything in the marquis' workshop was in perfect order. In one corner stood a training armature: an assembly of wood and rope meant to mimic the controls of an actual Cataphract, complete with a pair of spindly wooden arms tipped with grabbing claws. The whole contraption looked like some enormous, abstract marionette. Sturdy scaffolding was anchored to the walls, stretching upward, with various hoists and pulleys set up near the ceiling. On the ground level, workbenches lined the walls, polished tools hanging from rows upon rows of metal hooks.

Victor enviously inventoried the equipment on display. There were full sets of Cataphract wrenches, the smallest the thickness of his little finger, the largest as long as he was tall. Another workbench held a tangle of glass bottles and piping, suspended above charcoal burners by brass clamps. On the opposite side of the cavernous room, far away from any open flame, a grid of cubbyholes held tightly rolled sheets of paper and parchment. Victor's fingers twitched as he briefly fantasized about poring over the *Guilt of Gold*'s schematics. Just how old were those drawings? Could some of them stretch back to when she was first built, centuries ago? At university, he'd only been able to study copies of copies of copies (if he had been lucky). Just comparing the originals to one of its generational replicas would make for a fascinating several days of study in and of itself. At least it would, if Victor had the time.

"You're late."

Master Smith Marissa Chalment had swapped out her formal gown for a more practical shirt and trousers, accessorized with a blacksmith's heavy leather apron and gloves. Her golden hair was tied back in a simple bun, and the soot on her cheeks only reminded Victor how beautiful Marissa was.

"Am I?" Victor blurted. "My apologies."

"That's all right." Marissa smiled, sunny. "It's easy to get bogged down in the main house, especially when the marquis is putting something like this on. Makes me glad there's rooms on the third floor of the workshop for us engineers. Easy way to keep clear of all the commotion."

"Lucky you," Victor said.

"I suppose." Marissa shrugged. "But it can be a pain to walk all that way every time you have to run a message to the Marquis. Not that there's anything to say now, with the *Guilt of Gold* out in the gardens. But when we were actually working on it, the marquis wanted status reports every few hours, even when there wasn't anything to report. There's only so many ways to say 'we polished the machine's armor' without repeating yourself." Marissa rolled her eyes and went on. "But I suppose he's got a right to be particular about his Cataphract. It'd just be a lot more convenient if he could be bothered to come all the way down here and see for himself." She shook her head, then looked up at Victor. "But I'm rambling! The important part is that the marquis is happy with how the *Guilt of Gold* is running."

"As a prop," Victor said.

"As part of the marquis' ... entertainment, yes," Marissa said with a wince. "But what else is he supposed to do? The Brethren of the Chain haven't been a threat since the battle of Osterbridge, and there hasn't been a

Behemoth sighting for generations. And the marquis is far too smart to stick his nose into any border disputes between the Freeholder princes. Better that the marquis keep his Cataphract running, even if it's for trivial purposes, than let it sit idle and rust. In fact--" Marissa snapped her fingers as an idea came to mind. "Follow me. I want to show you something."

She led Victor across the floor of the workshop, through a set of large doors, and into a tight-packed storehouse. Boxes and barrels of every size were piled up and neatly labeled. The boxes contained everything needed to keep a Cataphract workshop running, from ingots of unworked steel to bottles of exotic, volatile chemicals safely packed away in straw. Marissa led Victor past the raw materials and to a more open stretch of the warehouse, where several large, cart-sized objects sat, covered by canvas.

"Take a look," Marissa said, and pulled the canvas back. Beneath was a Cataphract's arm--one from a duelist, to judge from its size. Pieces of its armor and the mechanisms underneath had been neatly removed, reminding Victor of a dissected lab specimen. Two of the hand's fingers were missing, and brown specks of rust marred the armor plating, like the first symptoms of rot. Victor ran his hand along the slightly dusty metal, then blinked as he saw the sigil of a stone tower etched into the back of the gauntlet.

"This is the *Stalwart*." He drew his hand back.

"What's left of her." Marissa gestured to the other canvas-draped hulks around them. "Her captain, Count Silvenet, died about three years ago. His son was supposed to take the helm next, but the boy was a useless rake. He spent all his time chasing skirts and playing cards, and left the *Stalwart* to rust. Even fired her crew so he wouldn't have to pay them. Marquis Maldrinne finally managed to take ownership of her in return for paying off some of the younger Silvenet's gambling debts, but he was too late." Marissa shook her head and draped the canvas back in place as if she were covering a dead body. In a way, she was. "Best we can do now is salvage what we can."

Victor walked over to another piece of the *Stalwart* and pulled the canvas back, revealing the machine's upper torso. Her visor had been removed, revealing the stripped-out gap of the Cataphract's helm-seat.

"What about her alchemical furnace?" Victor asked, looking over his shoulder. "So long as that's still working, the rest is just a matter of fabricating new parts."

"Which is an expensive process, even for someone as well off as the marquis," Marissa said. "But the furnace is intact, yes."

"So she could still walk again. Someday." Victor looked over the remnants of the *Stalwart*. Both legs and one had been removed, and in the cavity of the Cataphract's right knee, he saw the shine of brass. A set of motive gears was visible within the shoulder cavity, the mechanisms in pristine condition, and far easier to access than anything still inside the *Guilt of Gold*. In fact, if Marissa hadn't been there, Victor could have disconnected the motive gears with no trouble at all.

He bit the inside of his cheek to keep himself from saying something, anything, that would betray his intentions. Thankfully, Marissa took Victor's expression for something else entirely.

"I know how you feel." Marissa laid a gentle hand on Victor's arm, at which point he realized just how close the other alchemical engineer stood, and how brightly her hair shone even in the dim light of the warehouse. Suddenly, salvaging parts from the *Stalwart* seemed far, far less important. "It's hard, seeing a machine like this. After all that time studying how they work, and then to see someone just ... abandon it. Abandon her."

"I'd never--" Victor began, only to realize midway through the sentence that he wasn't sure if he was talking about Marissa or the *Stalwart*.

"I know." Marissa pulled canvas over the *Stalwart*'s torso once more. "I'm sorry. I shouldn't have started the tour here. It's depressing."

"That just means it's only going to get better?" Victor offered.

"Hah!" Marissa smacked him on the arm, hard enough to prove the Master Smith title was not unearned. "Ever the optimist. Now come on, we've still got the whole rest of the workshop to look at. The setup here is a lot different than the setup back at the university. Cleaner, for one. That, and it's a lot easier to manage working on a Cataphract when you don't have to worry about some idiot burning half the place down while trying to test their latest pet theory."

"Sounds lovely." Victor's laugh was forced, but Marissa didn't seem to notice.

Marissa led Victor through the warehouse again. When she opened the door leading back to the main workshop, Marquis Maldrinne was standing on the other side, along with a redheaded woman pressed up against his side. The marquis' companion let out a squeak of surprise and held a silk-gloved hand up to her mouth. Victor faintly remembered seeing the lady the night before, though then she'd been with the *Temper*'s captain. She must have liked Cataphracts, he decided.

"Master Smith Chalment! What a surprise!" Marquis Maldrinne said. "I should have known I'd find you here. Hard at work, I presume?"

"As always, sir." Marissa dipped into a polite curtsy, even though she was wearing trousers. Victor bowed as well, keeping his eyes respectfully downward, hoping madly that the marquis wouldn't recognize him.

"Good!" Marquis Maldrinne smiled. "As it happens, my good friend Baroness Pitchfell here had a few questions about Cataphracts, so I thought I might, ah--show her around."

"Of course, my lord," Marissa said. "I would be happy to give the both of you a tour, if you'd like."

"No, no." Marquis Maldrinne made a politely dismissive gesture with his hand. "I can handle things quite well myself. Especially when you appear to have company."

Victor gritted his teeth as he felt the marquis' eyes on him.

"As it would happen, I was showing Victor around the workshop, myself. We studied together at the university, you know." Marissa elbowed Victor lightly (at least, lightly by her standards) and he stood up straight.

"Did you, now?" The marquis narrowed his eyes, then leaned forward as he studied Victor's face until he snapped his fingers as the epiphany dawned on him. The waxed points of his mustache turned upward as he smiled. "So that's where we met! I knew you looked familiar, Journeyman Brinden. You're the one who nearly killed me!"

Marissa whipped her head around to stare at Victor. "You did what?"

"He didn't do it on purpose,but I'm not sure if that makes it better or worse. You should have seen it." Marquis Maldrinne shook his head and chuckled at the memory. "He was so proud of his precious experiment. That is, until it exploded. In front of the university's masters, to boot. And me, of course. An unmitigated disaster, I tell you. It's the sort of thing that makes one wonder just how prestigious the university really is, if a failure like him could make it so far. Then again, Master Smith Chalment, you're proof enough that at least someone there knows what they're doing."

Victor's cheeks flushed red, but he couldn't find the words to defend himself from the cold truth of his own failure.

"Things must work very differently at the university." Marquis Maldrinne's voice grew stern as he met Victor's eyes. "But here, in my domain, I think it's best that we keep the incompetents away from anything important. A misunderstanding such as this one can be forgiven. Once. As otherwise, well--were I a more paranoid man, I might think that my cousin Diana sent you here to sabotage something. She always did have a vicious streak. Never could take a joke."

"Sabotage?" Victor paled. He'd expected the marquis' aristocratic disdain, but the confused, suspicious expression on Marissa's face made his stomach twist into knots. "I-I'd never--"

"I know you wouldn't. But just to be sure." Marquis Maldrinne turned to Marissa and spoke with practiced, unquestionable authority. "Master Smith Chalment, I shall not risk this man endangering my birthright. He is not to be let back inside this building, or anywhere near the *Guilt of Gold*. As with all things concerning my Cataphract, I shall hold you personally responsible. See to it that he is removed at once. I'm sure we can find something shiny to distract him in the manor house proper."

"Understood, my lord." Marissa wrapped steely fingers around Victor's arm. "We were just on our way out."

"Excellent. Keep up the good work, Master Smith Chalment." The marquis nodded in approval, then guided his well-dressed companion into the warehouse while Marissa hauled Victor in the opposite direction. Victor stumbled to keep up with Marissa's pace as she dragged him through the workshop's main doors. She only released his arm once they were several yards away from the towering building, then jabbed Victor in the chest with two fingers, hard enough to rock him back on his heels.

"Mind explaining what that was about?" she demanded.

"It's as he said, I'm afraid." Victor rubbed the spot on his arm where Marissa had grabbed him and wondered if it would leave a bruise. "My thesis presentation didn't go as well as I'd planned, and unfortunately, he was there to witness it. But it wasn't quite as bad as he suggested?"

"And the other part? About some other idiot noble sending you to sabotage my work?"

"That's not why I'm here," Victor said.

"Then why are you here, Victor? Because right now it's looking damned suspicious that my employer's least favorite cousin has an alchemical engineer on her payroll. Especially one who's known for breaking things."

Victor winced at the reminder of his university failure. "It's--I mean, it's not--it's ... complicated."

"Complicated?" Marissa huffed. "Don't tell me you and Lady Fenvale are--"

"What?" Victor's cheeks flushed again. "No! It's not like that."

"It isn't?" Marissa took a step back and crossed her arms over her chest. "Then why did Lady Fenvale bring you in the first place? What's she planning?"

"I don't know," Victor said. It was even mostly true.

"You don't--" Marissa huffed out a frustrated breath and rubbed the bridge of her nose. "You don't even know what kind of trouble you've gotten yourself into. These aristocrats have nothing better to do than to play these stupid games, which means they take them very seriously. Which means that it's very easy for someone like you to get in too deep, and then the next thing you know, you're going to have to learn how to use one of those." She nodded to the rapier hanging at Victor's side.

"I could give you the same warning," Victor said. "Minus, er, the sword part, at least."

"I don't fence," Marissa said. "But I own a very fine set of pistols. And if you touch so much as a single bolt on the *Guilt of Gold*, I will show you just how accurate they are firsthand. Do you understand, Journeyman?"

Victor swallowed, despite his suddenly dry mouth. "Absolutely."

"Good." Marissa's shoulders slumped, her earlier threat already melting away. "Believe it or not, I'm trying to help you, Victor. You should get out of here while you still can. Go back to the university. Go back to your studies. Write a treatise or two. You might even be able to get Professor Dorrett to give you a stipend if you need the money."

"I can't do that," Victor said.

"And I can't let you sabotage one of my machines, all because of some idiot feud. Good day, Victor." Marissa squared her shoulders, turned on one heel, and walked back to the workshop. She barked a stern command to a few nearby apprentices, and the young men and women rushed to obey.

Marissa didn't bother looking back before the massive doors swung shut behind her.

CHAPTER 12

"You say my cousin was with a woman?" Lady Fenvale poured Victor a glass of wine to calm his rattled nerves. He'd initially been afraid to report his failed reconnaissance to her, but Lady Fenvale had listened to his story intently, and without any dark looks or barbed comments. In fact, Victor's account had made her smile, even if he wasn't sure why.

"Er, yes?" Victor said. "A baroness, I believe."

"With red hair?" Lady Fenvale leaned forward in her seat. "That'll be Baroness Pitchfell."

Victor gulped down a soothing mouthful of wine. "Is that relevant?"

"It's quite relevant," Lady Fenvale said. "In fact, it confirms a rumor I overheard last night. Which helps us considerably."

"How?" Victor blinked.

"You'll see soon enough." Lady Fenvale smiled and sipped at her wine. "And so will the rest of my cousin's guests. That'll give them something to talk about besides me."

Victor frowned. "I thought you didn't care about scandals and gossip? That you held yourself above that sort of thing?"

"I try to," Lady Fenvale said. "But I still grew up immersed in it. Every noblewoman does. And since my cousin made it a point to humiliate me with his little entertainment, I shall reply in kind."

"Don't tell me we came all this way just so you could spite the marquis."

"That's exactly why we came here," Lady Fenvale said. "It's just that we're going about it in a slightly different manner. But don't worry, I haven't forgotten about what we need. In fact, you may have the opportunity to get it very soon, depending on how things play out tonight."

"But I've been banned from the workshop. Master Smith Chalment threatened to shoot me."

"Master Smith Chalment will have bigger things to worry about before long." Lady Fenvale finished her wine and set the empty glass down on the table. "As will my cousin. While they're distracted, we shall acquire the parts you need. Can you salvage what you need from what's left of the *Stalwart*, instead of directly from the *Guilt of Gold*?"

"I could, yes," Victor said. "But--"

Lady Fenvale held up a hand, silencing him. "Then that's what we shall do. You've done good work, and you'll have more to do soon. But for now, there's nothing for us to do but wait and enjoy my cousin's hospitality. In fact, I have it on good authority that tonight's play should be quite ... distracting." She smiled her wolfish smile once again.

Victor wished he shared her confidence.

Dinner was served shortly before sunset, once again in the gardens behind Maldrinne House. Many of the guests were already pleasantly drunk from the day's polite revelry, so it took a little bit longer for everyone to settle down into their assigned seats. Once again, Victor sat between the same lady-in-waiting and horse master from the night before. Victor wished he'd thought to ask their names then. The rest of the seating was the same, though this time around, Marquis Maldrinne started the evening in his seat next to Lady Fenvale, instead of making a grand entrance via Cataphract. The *Guilt of Gold* still knelt behind the wooden stage, furnace unlit and dormant.

Victor also noted Baroness Pitchfell, the woman who had accompanied the marquis to the warehouse, was seated a few seats to the left of the Marquis. She sat next to a fiercely bearded man in a light blue tunic--Baron Pitchfell, he vaguely remembered. The *Temper*'s sigil, a snarling lion's head, marked him as a Cataphract captain.

Dinner was even more lavish than it had been the night before. Servants came bearing tray after tray of gourmet delicacies. Slabs of grilled salmon, smothered in herbs and butter. A massive wildfowl pie, made from layers of ornate, flaky pastry and stuffed with five different kinds of bird, as shown by the colorful feathers decorating the rim of the platter. Leg of mutton, slow-baked to the point where the meat fell from the bone at the slightest pressure. And for dessert, sliced, sugared pears drenched in brandy and briefly set aflame. The burning pears made something of a commotion, especially when some minor noble nearly set his mustache on fire. Instead of taking this as a warning, some of the drunker dinner guests were inspired to invent an impromptu game in which they tried to snatch slices of flaming fruit out of the serving bowl with their bare hands.

Victor watched the display and frowned. Marquis Maldrinne had mocked him for his disastrous experiment back at the university, yet saw nothing wrong with foisting burning fruit on his inebriated guests. Then again, hypocrisy seemed to be the chief privilege of the aristocracy.

Once everyone finished (or at least extinguished) their dessert, Carondel strutted out onstage to introduce his play. It took up shortly after where the last one had stopped and used most of the same tropes. Alice Renvallis found new ways to make a fool of herself, and the audience laughed at her--and at Lady Fenvale. Her face didn't turn quite as red as it had the night before, since this time she knew what was coming. That Marquis Maldrinne could sit next to her without getting stabbed was a show of bravery on his part and restraint on hers.

Soon, one of the actors ran in from the side of the stage, bearing a warning. A Behemoth had been sighted off the coast, headed right for the city. The characters bickered over who would fight the monster. Alice Renvallis volunteered repeatedly but was soon shouted down by the others on account of her lack of strength, skill, or common sense. After a few more creatively insulting couplets, the characters came to the inevitable conclusion that the nameless Errant Knight would be the one to face the monster. The characters turned to the audience, addressing Marquis Maldrinne directly as they went on to praise the bravery and prowess of the Errant Knight. The marquis basked in the verbose flattery, until Carondel himself walked out onstage, clad in yellow and red motley and carrying a lute. The playwright took a deep breath before delivering his lines with gusto.

"By the moon and stars above,

"The Errant Knight fights for love!"

Knight-Colonel Renvallis gasped and raised a hand to his mustache-framed mouth in shock.

"Our knight? In love? Could it be true?

"Surely you can tell us-- who?"

The playwright smiled and turned to deliver his lines directly to the audience instead of the other actors on stage:

"No other beauty can compare

"To her snowy skin and flame-red hair.

"Her eyes are pools that gleam so deep,

"That there's no end to the secrets they might keep.

"And yet, she's more than just a pretty sight.

"She's clever too, and oh so bright.

"Her wit is sharp, her voice a song.

"Her heart is kind, and virtue strong."

As Carondel spoke, the audience's attention shifted away from the stage and to the red-haired baroness sitting in the next row. Baroness Pitchfell blushed and fanned herself, feigning ignorance, even as the play flattered her at length. Victor looked back to Lady Fenvale. She sipped casually at her wine, but Victor still saw her wolfish smile behind the rim of her goblet.

The play went on, and so did Carondel:

"Her only flaw, so it be said

"Is that the lady is promis'd to wed,

"Not by choice, but by duty.

"For a wicked count did crave her beauty.

"Beneath his silken sash and tailored coat,

"He is, in truth, a surly goat

"Who threatened to cast her family down

"Unless she donned a wedding gown.

"Sorrow was to be her fate,

"Until this most auspicious date.

"As here's a man to solve her plight--

"That great hero--our Errant Knight!"

Carondel took a breath to continue his monologue, but a cry from the audience cut him off.

"Enough!"

Face mirroring the snarling lion on his tunic, Baron Pitchfell sprang to his feet. The man's face went crimson, and livid veins bulged from his temples. "Did you really think you could ... could slander me like this? And worse yet, you insult my wife with your saccharine nonsense. I don't care if you're the host or not. This cannot stand!" He pulled off his left dress glove, then threw the scrap of white cloth into Marquis Maldrinne's face. The glove bounced from the marquis' cheek and fell to the table.

Baron Pitchfell continued his red-faced ranting. "Since you're so happy to show off your Cataphract, I shall give you the opportunity for a proper demonstration. Unless you'd prefer to settle accounts tonight?" He set a hand on his sword, then raised his eyebrows in question. A murmur spread through the audience, and Victor saw Rochen Dunsall and several other of the marquis' men reach for their own blades, ready to defend their employer.

Marquis Maldrinne stood, tall and dignified in his black formal wear and gold-hilted dress sword. "So this is how you repay my hospitality?" he sneered. "If you've found my accommodations wanting, you're welcome to leave. But there's nothing to be mad about. There's no reason to get worked up over a trifling entertainment like--"

Baron Pitchfell's fingers tightened around the hilt of his sword. "Swords or Cataphracts. Answer me, or I'll cut you down here and now."

Rochen Dunsall started shoving his way through the audience, hand on the hilt of his rapier, but he stopped when Marquis Maldrinne waved him off.

"Very well." Marquis Maldrinne kept his voice even. "Go, then. If you still have quarrel with me by the time you get back to the *Temper*, bring her here and I'll see to your satisfaction."

The bearded count nodded--if not in approval, then at least in agreement--and stormed out of the audience. Baroness Pitchfell stared, aghast, but she didn't follow her husband. As soon as the baron disappeared from sight, the rest of the audience started murmuring among themselves, having entirely forgotten the drama onstage in favor of the scandal that had just played out before them. Marquis Maldrinne only stoked the flames of rumor as he left without comment, heading back to the main house-- as Baroness Pitchfell followed.

At that, the rest of the marquis' guests left their seats, streaming down to the garden and stage in order to gather together in little groups and exchange gossip. Everyone seemed to have some new theory, based on some tiny observation. They wondered about the origin of the jewelry Baroness Pitchfell wore, or how close Marquis Maldrinne's hand was to his sword, or even possible hidden meaning behind the dishes served for dinner. Meanwhile, Marissa, still clad in a fine gown, hitched up her skirts and took off in the direction of her workshop. Remembering her earlier threat, Victor gave the master smith and her assistants a wide berth and kept his mouth shut. The other guests were happy to ignore him. After all, who would pay attention to a failure of an alchemical engineer when there was a Cataphract duel looming?

Amid the gossip and commotion, Victor watched Carondel and his actors frantically stuff their costumes and props into bags and trunks before hauling their baggage off towards the stables as fast as they could manage. Nobody had thought to pin the scandal on Carondel yet, and the playwright no doubt wanted to escape before somebody did.

Victor wished he could join them.

CHAPTER 13

"He's going to kill him." Lady Fenvale said. "Or maybe the baron will just wound him a little. Either way, it should be a worth watching."

Again, she paced back and forth in the suite, though this time her restless energy was far less frustrated than it had been the previous morning. Again, the marquis' servants had brought in a breakfast platter, and again Victor didn't eat much of it. The previous night's feasting still sat heavy in his stomach, doing no favors for his anxiety. Lady Fenvale, of course, showed no such discomfort and took a slice of orange or morsel of cheese from the platter each time she passed.

"It's perfect. First, we get to watch the *Temper* beat the hell out of the *Guilt of Gold*. Afterwards, we can get what we need while they're repairing my cousin's Cataphract, without anyone noticing. It'll be easier to explain a missing part after a battle than before one. This way, we can take something from the *Guilt of Gold* or the *Stalwart*, depending on which is easier."

"But what if the marquis doesn't lose?" Victor asked. "What if the *Guilt of Gold* comes through unscathed, and there aren't any repairs necessary?"

"You're an alchemical engineer, Victor. You should know, more than anyone, how much maintenance a machine that size requires."

"Good point," Victor admitted.

"Besides, my father once went on campaign alongside the *Temper*. She's a fine machine, and Baron Pitchfell captains her well."

"That's no guarantee he'll win."

Lady Fenvale stopped her pacing and frowned. "Perhaps," she admitted. "But he'll still make a good account of himself, which will give us an opportunity."

"Assuming Baron Pitchfell doesn't calm down and stay home."

"Ah." Lady Fenvale held up a finger. "The *Temper* is very aptly named. Baron Pitchfell will come, I know."

"Did you know that he'd react the way he did? The baron, that is."

"I didn't expect him to react so quickly, to be honest," Lady Fenvale said. "Suits me fine all the same."

"And you're all right with this? With forcing the man into a duel with your cousin?"

"Victor." Lady Fenvale stopped her pacing and turned to stare intently at the engineer. "I did not force the baron into anything. Moreover, you saw my cousin and Baroness Pitchfell together. And if you saw them, that means that countless others did, as well. If Marquis Maldrinne wants to dally with another man's wife, he should expect the consequences. It was only a matter of time before Pritchfell found out, and only a matter of time before he challenged my cousin for it. I simply helped matters along."

"'Helped' isn't the word I would use. 'Incited' seems more accurate."

"Why do you care?"

"Because this isn't what I signed up for." Victor surprised himself as he said it. Still, he kept talking, spurred on by his anxiety. "I'm only an alchemical engineer. Not a spy, or a thief, or whatever it is you expect from me. I'm not suited for any of this, this--skullduggery. And I thought you weren't, either, but here you are scheming and plotting just like the rest of them."

Lady Fenvale stepped back, as if struck. Victor braced himself for her blistering reply, but instead, she closed her eyes and took in a deep breath before she spoke.

"I'm sorry." She sat down in the chair opposite Victor. "If it's any consolation, this hasn't been exactly pleasant for me, either. Ever since my cousin had that damned play put on, every groveling lickspittle who wants to get into his good graces has been making little barbs and jests at my expense. You haven't been present for most of it. And even if you were, you might not even realize it. For example, did you notice the other noblewomen wearing white gloves last night?"

"I hadn't thought to look."

Lady Fenvale held up her own ungloved hand and flexed her

fingers, tendons moving beneath her light brown skin. "Exactly. If you don't know what to look for, it's invisible. Just another quirk of fashion. But if you know the meaning behind it--"

"Which is?"

"Soft gloves mean soft hands. Unlike mine." Lady Fenvale rubbed her thumb across her fingertips, over the calluses she'd built up from untold hours of fencing practice.

"Are you sure?" Victor asked. "Maybe it is just another little quirk of fashion?"

"There's no question of it, Victor. Baroness Pitchfell told me directly, right before she 'generously' offered to give me some of her old dresses so I would have something more 'appropriate' to wear." She spat. "I declined, of course. It's bad enough that they think I'm a brute, but if I start accepting their so-called charity? Bah. I'd rather be a badly dressed pariah than someone's sycophant."

"Ah." Victor took in Lady Fenvale's plain but well-tailored gown. "If it's any consolation, I don't see anything wrong with what you're wearing. It suits you quite well."

"Thank you. Unfortunately, not everyone shares your opinion." Lady Fenvale got to her feet and started pacing again. "I've had to deal with these kinds of insults for years, Victor. If it's not gloves, it's fans, or hats, or some other useless bit of frippery that arbitrarily distinguishes who's popular and who isn't. And since I can't challenge Baroness Pitchfell and her ilk to a duel, I'm forced to resort to more indirect tactics. Thankfully, we won't have to worry about them for much longer. Give it another week, and we'll be marching the *Huntress* to Kingsforge. Once I swear the Cataphract Oath, everyone's going to look at my sigil instead of my gloves." She reached up with her right hand and patted a spot over her left breast.

Outside, someone sounded a bugle. Lady Fenvale perked up, then tilted her head to listen to the signal. "And that's Baron Pitchfell. Better find a good place to watch." She picked up a leather bag from where she'd left it on a chair, slung the strap over her shoulder, and headed out into the hall. Victor followed, awkwardly belting his rapier on as he hurried to keep up with Lady Fenvale's long, confident stride. They weren't the only ones who'd heard the bugle, either. Within minutes, the hallways of Maldrinne House were crowded with guests and staff, all trying to find a position near a window or at least a way to get outside.

Lady Fenvale opted for the latter and headed out through the front doors and into the open air. The marquis' staff had set up tall canvas awnings and long, refreshment-laden tables, as if for a picnic. Lady Fenvale ignored the food and drink and instead walked a short distance from the crowd to give herself a clear line of sight. The valley stretched out before them, lush and green, and at the other end, rounding the pass, was the *Temper*.

She was a sleek, impressive machine, with steel armor tinted to a cobalt blue. The *Temper* carried an enormous halberd, its haft the length and thickness of a tall-ship mast. The hooked blade of the polearm was made from the same blued metal as the *Temper*'s armor and gleamed in the sun. A small squadron of horsemen followed the Cataphract--engineers, scouts, and other members of Baron Pitchfall's retinue. Lady Fenvale took a brass telescope from her bag to get a better look at them.

"What do you think?" After a minute or two's observation, Lady Fenvale handed her telescope to Victor. He sighted in on the *Temper*, watching her move down the valley. Squinting through the telescope, Victor sized the machine up with an engineer's eye, grateful to focus on something he actually knew about instead of gossip and intrigue. As the *Temper* marched down the valley, a lookout on the manor house's roof blew on a bugle again, announcing the impending arrival of the *Temper*, in case anyone had missed it the first time.

Victor lowered the telescope. "The *Temper* moves well, which means Baron Pitchfell has a good alchemical engineer on staff. She's fairly light for a duelist, which means she's fast, but not as heavily armored as the *Guilt of Gold*. Which is what the halberd is for--greater reach lets Baron Pitchfell keep his distance."

Lady Fenvale nodded. "If Baron Pitchfell can use that hook on the back of the blade to trip the *Guilt of Gold*, it's as good as over."

"Something tells me it's not going to be nearly that easy," Victor said.

Another bugle sounded, this one from the rear of the house. The ground rumbled, and the crowd gathered on the lawn and on the balconies cheered as the *Guilt of Gold* ponderously strode into view. Marquis Maldrinne had the visor open, and he waved to his guests from the helm-seat, as if the impending duel was just another part of the midsummer festivities. In a way, one could argue it was. With her massive broadsword balanced on one shoulder, the *Guilt of Gold* strode forward. Some of the braver (or at least more inebriated) among the marquis' guests followed in her wake, clapping and cheering. Lady Fenvale stayed where she was, content to watch from a distance.

The *Temper* and the *Guilt of Gold* met in a long flat field at the bottom of the valley. Each Cataphract's entourage clustered behind their chosen machine: hard-faced horsemen on one side and laughing revelers on the other. One of the horsemen from Baron Pitchfell's retinue dismounted and walked to the middle of the field, where one of Marquis Maldrinne's men met him.

Lady Fenvale took up the telescope so she could watch the two men in the middle of the field. "He's got his pet bastard, Rochen, acting as his second. There's no way this will end quietly now. My cousin probably told Dunsall to insult him again, just for good measure."

"Why would he do that?"

"This whole festival is just his excuse to show off how rich and important he is. My cousin might not have planned on a duel, but he'll still use the opportunity to show off. It'd be damned anticlimactic if the seconds were to negotiate a peace, especially now that Baron Pitchfell's called my cousin's bluff. Which is why he sent Dunsall. I don't think I've met anyone so good at being an ass."

Lady Fenvale's theory proved correct when the man speaking with Rochen Dunsall threw down his hat and stormed back to the *Temper*. Dunsall ambled back to the *Guilt of Gold* with a swagger in his step. Marquis Maldrinne closed the *Guilt of Gold*'s visor, and the Cataphract hoisted her sword up into the air in salute. The *Temper* closed her visor in turn, then took the haft of her halberd in both hands and lowered the point into fighting position, aimed right at the *Guilt of Gold*'s midsection.

The duel was on.

The thunder of heavy footfalls and the clanking of armor drowned out the audience's cheering as the machines closed in. The *Guilt of Gold* held her broadsword with both hands, angled out in front of her, but the *Temper*'s polearm still gave her greater reach. The *Temper* opened with a series of quick, shallow thrusts, testing her opponent's guard. Steel rang on steel as the *Guilt of Gold* parried once, twice, but the third got past her guard. The halberd's spike hit the *Guilt of Gold*'s shoulder and glanced off her left pauldron. The point only scratched the armor without any lasting damage, but a murmur passed through the audience all the same.

"Serves him right." Lady Fenvale spoke more to herself than to Victor.

The *Temper* pressed her advantage. The hook on the back of her halberd caught on the *Guilt of Gold*'s shoulder armor, and the *Temper* yanked the larger Cataphract off-balance. The *Guilt of Gold* staggered but didn't fall, riposting with a quick thrust. The *Temper* parried, then swung the butt end of her halberd up to hit the *Guilt of Gold* just beneath the visor.

The cloud of alchemical smoke belching from the *Guilt of Gold*'s exhaust vents grew thicker as Marquis Maldrinne pushed her alchemical furnace harder. The black-armored Cataphract locked the crossguard of her broadsword with the haft of the *Temper*'s halberd and heaved, forcing the weapon upwards. The *Guilt of Gold* stepped inside her opponent's guard and slammed a shoulder into the *Temper*'s breastplate, hard enough to dent the metal. Only Baron Pitchfell's expert piloting kept his machine on her feet as she reeled drunkenly backward. The *Temper* twisted at the waist and planted the butt of her halberd into the ground to steady herself, then pushed off to meet the *Guilt of Gold*'s next attack.

The two Cataphracts laid into each other with blow after savage blow, and the din of clashing metal echoed through Maldrinne Valley. Armor plating bent beneath the heavy blades, but neither war machine could land a decisive blow on the other. The *Guilt of Gold*'s armor was too thick, while the *Temper*'s greater speed allowed her to dodge the other's attacks. But with each narrow miss, the *Temper* was forced back another step or two, to the point where Baron Pitchfell's entourage had to take to their horses and scatter in order to avoid getting crushed. As Marquis Maldrinne gained ground, his guests cheered and downed preemptive toasts to his impending victory.

The *Temper* whipped her halberd around after a parry, then lunged. The spiked head of the polearm punched through a gap in the *Guilt of Gold*'s armor where her right leg met her torso. The high-pitched twang of snapping control cables rang out as the halberd blade sank in deeper. The toasts petered off to silence.

Lady Fenvale smiled. With teeth.

Even with one leg crippled, the *Guilt of Gold* fought on. One massive hand wrapped around the shaft of her opponent's weapon, holding it still so she could bring her sword down with the other. The blade hit true, shattering the treated lumber of the *Temper*'s halberd, leaving the wagon-sized blade embedded in her hip joint. The broadsword rose up on the backswing, catching the *Temper* beneath the left elbow, shearing through the joint in a single blow. The heavy gauntlet hit the ground, trailing snapped lengths of control cable. The *Temper* soon followed suit, smashed into the ground by the flat of her opponent's sword.

The *Guilt of Gold* limped forward, still mobile enough to plant her good foot on the *Temper*'s dented breastplate. Both hands took hold of the broadsword's hilt once again, reversing the blade to point directly at the *Temper*'s visor hatch, poised for a killing blow.

The *Temper*'s visor flipped open, and Baron Pitchfell's pained yell could be heard even at Maldrinne House.

"I yield!"

More cheering rose up from the marquis' guests. More uncorked bottles. More toasts. The celebration soon got into full swing, even as gray clouds began to move in above, casting the valley in shadow.

Lady Fenvale put her telescope back into her bag and pressed her lips into a thin, disciplined line. She caught Victor by the arm, pulling him in close so they couldn't be overheard amid the celebration surrounding them. "This doesn't change anything," she said, though Victor wasn't sure if it was for his benefit or hers. "We can still go through with the rest of the plan."

"But not now, right?" Victor kept his voice low. "I mean, everyone's still watching."

"I didn't say immediately." Lady Fenvale looked down at her fingers on Victor's arm, and slowly released her grip before turning back to the manor house. "We should get back to the suite and--" Her eyes went wide, and her words trailed off. Victor blinked, then turned to follow Lady Fenvale's gaze only to find none other than Rochen Dunsall standing between them and the house.

"You're not cheering, Lady Fenvale," he noted.

"I must be short of breath," she replied coolly. "A lady's constitution can be delicate, you know. I think I shall take a stroll in the rear gardens. Get some air where it's less crowded."

"Under normal circumstances, I would be more than happy to escort you myself." Dunsall's faux-friendly tone made Victor's stomach churn. "But the marquis wishes to speak with you."

"And if I do not wish to speak with him?" Lady Fenvale took a step closer to Victor--not for protection, but so she could get her hand near the rapier hanging from his side.

"He was quite insistent." Dunsall examined the fingernails of his right hand, while the left rested comfortably on the hilt of his sword. "Which is why he didn't send me alone."

Victor swallowed and looked around. Sure enough, a loose ring of Maldrinne's men surrounded them, their hands conspicuously close to their weapons. They ostensibly drank and chatted with the other guests, but the way they were stationed to cut off any potential route of escape was anything but coincidental. Lady Fenvale drew in a seething breath as she realized her tactical position, or lack thereof.

"In that case." Lady Fenvale hooked her arm through Victor's elbow, then tilted her chin proudly upward, refusing to be cowed. "Lead the way."

CHAPTER 14

Dunsall escorted Lady Fenvale and Victor away from the celebration; nobody appeared to notice or care about their absence. Victor feared he'd be thrown into some cellar or dungeon, but was pleasantly surprised when they were taken to the marquis' study instead.

The study's walls were lined with tall hardwood bookcases, which held neat rows of books. With no small degree of annoyance, Victor realized the books had been arranged merely by size and the color of their binding, instead of by subject. Which is to say, they weren't organized at all. A first edition of Principles of Ambulatory Motion sat next to last year's printing of A Theoretical Taxonomy of Aquatic Behemoths, which in turn sat next to the infamously salacious (and occasionally banned) novel, Lady Undile's Predilections.

"Your sword, please." Dunsall caught Victor by the arm and nodded to a trio of leather upholstered armchairs at the center of the room. "It'll be easier for you to sit without it getting in the way, friend."

Victor looked down to the rapier at his hip. The weapon had been nothing but an awkward, heavy burden, but the prospect of losing it hardly appealed either. Still, seeing no other choice, Victor shrugged out of the baldric and handed over the still-sheathed sword. Dunsall accepted it, then gave the weapon to one of his henchmen stationed in the corner. With Victor disarmed, Dunsall went on with the polite fiction of the visit, as if he hadn't brought them in under threat of force. "The marquis should be along shortly. I can have refreshments brought up, if you like."

"That's quite unnecessary, thank you." Lady Fenvale eased herself into a chair and nodded for Victor to do the same. She played along, meeting Dunsall's politeness with a frosty smile of her own. "Do you know how long he'll be?"

"As soon as he can get away from everyone wishing to congratulate him on his victory." He shrugged. "It may be a while."

"Then there's nothing to do but wait," Lady Fenvale said.

And that's what they did.

Outside, the marquis' guests celebrated his victory, their cheers and laughter carrying through the study's open windows. Victor ignored them and occupied himself by mentally reorganizing the marquis' bookshelves. It'd be a trivial matter to separate the histories from the treatises on philosophy, and even to quarantine the more salacious works on the top shelf where impressionable children couldn't reach them. He doubted the marquis would actually allow him to reorganize the study, but the exercise kept him from thinking about what would happen next. Victor supposed it was a good sign that they'd been brought to the study, and not someplace more unpleasant. Even if the shelves weren't organized properly, Marquis Maldrinne obviously took enough pride in his library that he wouldn't risk staining the expensive carpets and furniture with blood.

Then again, the presence of Dunsall and his men was a clear indication that this was no casual chat. And with the chairs at the center of the room, it would be far too easy for one of his men to creep up behind Victor with drawn knife and--

Victor focused on the shelves again.

After three-quarters of an hour, the marquis arrived, still wearing the padded protective jacket of a Cataphract captain. His hair was mussed, but he smiled all the same as he flopped down into the chair opposite Lady Fenvale and Victor. He snapped his fingers, and one of his men hurried over with a fresh glass of wine.

"So, dear Cousin, have you enjoyed your stay thus far? This Summer's Steel festival is proving even more eventful than I thought it would. Thanks to you."

"I'm glad to be of service," Lady Fenvale said, droll and deadpan.

"Oh, but you have been of service." Marquis Maldrinne leaned forward in his seat. "I've been wanting to have a go at the *Temper* for a while now. People were saying she was better built than the *Guilt of Gold*. Something about furnaces or joints or other technical details. I wasn't planning on things playing out so soon, but ... Well, I wasn't planning on you attending this festival to begin with. The last time you came it was only because Lady Rosalind had dragged you along, and that was years and years ago.

"That's how I knew you were planning some kind of scandal. I thought you'd stab someone, or send your saboteur there to make things difficult for my engineers. But goading Baron Pitchfell into challenging me? That's surprisingly devious, dear Cousin. I didn't think you had it in you." The marquis leaned back in his chair, smiling.

"I pride myself on my unpredictability," Lady Fenvale said.

"Getting Carondel to change his stupid play at the last moment was a nice touch. Dunsall got the full story out of the little man before he left. But there's one thing I haven't been able to figure out yet. How did you forge my seal?" He took a folded sheet of paper out of his pocket and let it fall open, revealing a hastily penned letter detailing the new outline to Carondel's play. The marquis' coin-and-dagger sigil, pressed in red wax, sat on the bottom of the letter, making it official correspondence.

"I used a hot knife to lift the seal off the invitation you sent, then applied it to a blank piece of paper." She nodded to the letter in the marquis' hand. "Seemed to be a fitting irony."

"Clever. And here I was afraid you'd somehow stolen into my offices when no one was looking." Marquis Maldrinne dropped the letter, and it floated down to the carpet. "Honestly, the worst part of this whole affair is that Baroness Pitchfell is now convinced that I'm actually in love with her." He shook his head. "Just yesterday, she was perfectly content to dally and leave it at that, but between the play and the duel, she's turned into a lovestruck schoolgirl. It's embarrassing."

"How unfortunate," said Lady Fenvale.

"Which is why I didn't kill Baron Pitchfell. If I'd widowed the baroness, it'd only be a matter of time before she flung herself at me. If her husband's still alive, that should keep her occupied--with trying to get a divorce, if nothing else."

"What if the baron holds a grudge?" Lady Fenvale asked. "Most men don't take well to being cuckolded. What's to stop him from challenging you again? Or acting against you some other way?"

"Baron Pitchfell owes me his life; he won't forget that anytime soon. Furthermore, if he starts making too much trouble, I can always tell him who really told Carondel to change the play." He nudged the letter on the floor with his boot. "Pitchfell's a man of honor, a traditionalist. Which means he'd never challenge a woman to a duel. He'd have to settle for a man in your immediate vicinity."

Victor squirmed beneath Marquis Maldrinne's cool gaze, but remained quiet.

"Your taste in champions is lacking, Cousin," he continued. "But at least this milksop can lift a sword, unlike your father these days."

Lady Fenvale's body tensed, but she did not lunge for her cousin's throat. Yet. "My father is twice the man you'll ever be."

"Not anymore, he's not." The marquis leaned back in his seat.

"What are you talking about?"

"My contacts have informed me that your father has sent for a physician. Given how stubborn he is, I imagine things must be quite bad if it's gotten that far. In fact, I wouldn't be surprised if we got news of his passing by the end of the festival."

"Liar," Lady Fenvale growled.

"Believe it or not, Cousin, I'm not lying. And even if I were, we both know your father isn't well. It's only a matter of time before he passes and I inherit the countship. Which is why I suggest you listen to my offer."

"I'm not interested." Lady Fenvale sank down into her tall chair like a cornered wolf in its den.

Marquis Maldrinne went on. "While it's true you've made things inconvenient for me, you've also shown me that you're a woman of drive. Of cunning. Of willpower. I could use a woman like you on my side. You've given me this much trouble with little more than an invitation and a failed engineering student--just think of what you'd be capable of in the courts and salons of Kingsforge, with proper backing. With proper purpose. Or if you'd prefer a life of more direct action, you could just buckle on a sword and ride with Dunsall the next time he runs his errands."

Rochen Dunsall stifled a spiteful laugh.

Lady Fenvale didn't bother looking at him, instead focusing her seething anger on her cousin. "Why would I ever work for you?"

"Because it'd be beneficial to the both of us. I get a capable lieutenant, and you would be comfortably compensated for it. After all, when I ascend to a higher title, I could recommend a worthy successor to take my old one." Marquis Maldrinne steepled his fingers in front of his pointed mustache. "Marquise Fenvale has a certain ring to it, don't you think?"

Lady Fenvale kept her mouth pressed into a thin, neutral line. "Do you really think you can bribe me?"

Instead of answering the question, Marquis Maldrinne turned to face Victor. "Tell me, Journeyman Brinden. Why are Cataphracts built in the shape of men?"

"Th-there are differing schools of thought," Victor offered, and nervously pushed his glasses further up his nose. While Victor cringed to have so many people (most of them armed) focusing on him, the opportunity to talk about something he actually knew about was comforting. "The first is somewhat philosophical. Namely, it posits that Leon, the first Cataphract King, was divinely inspired, and as such Cataphracts take their form to match the perfection of mankind."

Much to Victor's surprise, Lady Fenvale and Marquis Maldrinne both listened intently as he went into the theory. He tried not to let the attention distract him as he went on.

"The other, more practical--and honestly more popular--opinion is that, by mirroring the shape of a person, two arms, two legs, and so on, one can apply certain principles of anatomy and medicine to the construction and maintenance of the Cataphract. Control cables instead of tendons, an alchemical furnace instead of a heart; the parallels aren't perfect, but they're close enough. Moreover, such a layout makes the controls more intuitive. A skilled captain can utilize fencing techniques and principles that they've learned outside of the helm."

"You're close, but you're not thinking big enough," said Marquis Maldrinne. "A Cataphract isn't meant to be a symbol of perfection, simply because men are far from perfect."

"So I've noticed," said Lady Fenvale.

Marquis Maldrinne ignored his cousin and continued, "Moreover, there's hardly anything practical about a machine that complicated. No, Journeyman Brinden, I've realized there's only one reason to build a Cataphract to look like a man: power." He savored the word like wine on his tongue.

"That's certainly one way to look at it. The bipedal design does have some influence on the output of the alchemical furnace--" Victor prattled on.

"You need to stop thinking like an engineer," Marquis Maldrinne said. "Hell, with the way your demonstration went, you should never have started thinking like an engineer. I'm not talking about a furnace's output, I'm talking about power. A Cataphract is an extension of the man at the helm, and a man captaining a Cataphract is capable of anything. Which means I am capable of anything. Everyone who looks at the *Guilt of Gold* knows how much I've accomplished and is given a promise of what I can do in the future. My machine proves I am destined for greatness--though my cousin doesn't want to admit it."

"Please." Lady Fenvale rolled her eyes. "You inherited your title, your Cataphract, and more money than you'll ever be able to spend. There's nothing accomplished about that."

"Don't envy my birthright, Cousin. Having been given so much only means I have a responsibility to make best use of it. It's a lesson you could stand to learn yourself, or do you intend to spend your whole life making mine more difficult?"

"It's more appealing than being your lackey," Lady Fenvale said curtly.

Marquis Maldrinne leaned forward, steepling his fingers in front of his face. "Consider my offer, Cousin. Because when your father dies-- which he will, sooner rather than later--I can make things quite unpleasant for you. Once your father's holdings come into my possession, I would be well within my rights to liquidate them. It'd be easy to sell the manor house, have that beastly dog of yours shot, and turn that doddering old sergeant your father keeps around out into the street, provided he doesn't keel over when your father does. As for you, I'm sure I could find someone desperate enough to marry you. Maybe some fat merchant looking to marry into a title. I'm certain you'd wind up murdering him, running away, or both, but by then it'd be none of my concern. I'm sure it'd be entertaining, though."

"You're making a compelling argument for me to kill you right now." Lady Fenvale's voice dripped with sarcasm, but she curled her fingers slightly, reflexively, as if yearning to close them around the hilt of a sword--or her cousin's throat.

"Spare me the bravado." The marquis waved a dismissive hand at Lady Fenvale. "Any satisfaction you'd get from killing me would be short-lived, and you know it. Unless you think you can slaughter a half dozen of my best men with nothing but your bare hands?"

"It could be worth finding out," Lady Fenvale said.

"You haven't tried yet." Marquis Maldrinne leaned back in his chair. "Which implies you're considering my offer on some level. So be reasonable, Cousin. I'm more than willing to offer you terms. Quite generous ones, I might add. I'm also quite willing to ruin you, along with everything you've ever loved, just to prove my point. So the choice is yours, Diana."

Lady Fenvale narrowed her eyes. "I--"

Marquis Maldrinne held up a hand before Lady Fenvale could launch into curses and invective. "You're angry. I understand that. Which is why I'm going to give you some time to consider my generosity." He snapped his fingers. "Dunsall, see to it that my cousin and her assistant are returned to their quarters. Then post men at the door to make sure she's not disturbed. I expect the celebrations may grow somewhat raucous this evening, and I would not wish Lady Fenvale to be caught up in anything untoward."

Dunsall nodded, then took up a position a sword's length away from Lady Fenvale's chair. "Shall we, my lady?"

"If I might make a request, Cousin." The marquis drained his goblet. "Don't abuse my hospitality, at least no more than you have already. I'd hate to lock you away in the basement like a common ruffian. As we can both agree that you're anything but common."

Rochen Dunsall and his men escorted Lady Fenvale and Victor back to their suite and locked the door from the outside. With most of the marquis' guests still celebrating his victory on the front lawn, at least there wasn't anyone to gawk at the tableau of Lady Fenvale being essentially taken prisoner. Again, Victor supposed the suite was better than some rat-infested oubliette, just to look on the optimistic side of things.

"You were right, Victor. This is a disaster." Without anyone to direct her anger at, Lady Fenvale's energy drained away. Her shoulders slumped as she sat down at the suite's small table and held her face in her hands. "We never should have come here. We're stuck here, while my father is--"

"--going to be proud of you?" Victor winced as soon as the inadequate words left his mouth. As he watched Lady Fenvale sit and shrink in on herself, he knew he had to say something, though he had no idea what, exactly. People were complicated, Lady Fenvale even more so.

"Proud? What do I have to be proud of?" Lady Fenvale wiped at her eyes, hurriedly, as if to make sure Victor couldn't see the tears welling up there. "Of failure? Of getting blackmailed? Either I let my cousin ruin me, or I agree to be his--his stooge. And that's assuming he's made the offer in good faith. This could just be another of his sick games. For all I know he's just looking for a new way to humiliate me. To hurt me. To hurt--I swear, if he so much as touches Lily, I'll--"

"At least the marquis didn't gloat about stripping the *Huntress* for parts?" Victor grasped at the tiniest threads of optimism. "It'd be a damned waste after everything we've done up to this point, which seems to fit the marquis' style, for lack of a better word."

Lady Fenvale blinked tears from her eyes, then turned her head towards Victor. Slowly, gradually, Lady Fenvale's lips once again turned upwards into a knowing, lupine grin. "You're right, Victor."

"I should hope so?" Victor said. "I mean, I worked on that Cataphract for weeks, and if she were scrapped for lack of motive gears--"

"Not that, the other part." Lady Fenvale stood up again and started pacing the room, her booted footsteps deliberately loud in the small guest suite. She started speaking more quietly, which was when Victor realized someone might be eavesdropping now that they were held prisoner. "My cousin never mentioned the *Huntress* at all. He still doesn't know the real reason we're here. We can use that."

"We can?"

"If I get you those gears, you can fix the *Huntress*. If you can fix the *Huntress*, my cousin won't have any more leverage over me, even if my father is--"

"Fine?" Victor reached out hesitantly and patted Lady Fenvale on the shoulder. Again, optimism. "I mean, given the marquis' cruelty, he couldn't resist gloating if your father were--"

"Stop talking, Victor." Lady Fenvale smiled as she said it. "I've wasted enough time already. We need to act quickly. While Marquis Maldrinne is still gloating, we've got an opening."

"An opening?" Victor furrowed his brow as the realization hit him. "Wait, are you saying--"

"That's right, we can still get those motive gears after all." Lady

Fenvale rubbed her hands together. "But we're going to have to do it tonight."

CHAPTER 15

Night fell.

A rainstorm rolled in, forcing the revelers to take cover inside the spacious halls of Maldrinne House. Music and laughter echoed through the building, the sounds of celebration audible even in Lady Fenvale's suite at the far end of the house.

Not that there was anyone there to hear it.

Victor tightened his grip on the rope of tied-together blankets. In principle, the three-story drop wasn't that much taller than the heights he'd ascended to (and descended from) while working on the *Huntress*. Then again, even his rickety, thrown-together scaffolding was more stable than the line of wool and linen he dangled from, and the Cataphract's armor provided far more traction to his boots than the rain-slick statuary decorating the exterior of Maldrinne House. Victor focused on the taut bedding rope, marking his progress by each component. Wool blanket. Linen bedsheet. Embroidered quilt. After about a year's descent, Victor's boots touched the blessedly solid ground, and he let himself breathe again.

"Took you long enough," Lady Fenvale said from her lurking spot in the shadow of the manor wall. She had changed into a dark gray doublet and trousers, far more suitable for skullduggery than her formal gown. A wide-brimmed hat kept the rain out of Lady Fenvale's face, and Victor found himself wishing he had one to match. Changing clothes (and belting on a long dagger) had revitalized her; Lady Fenvale stood taller and moved with more purpose than she had since arriving at Maldrinne House. Not for the first time, Victor wished he shared her easy confidence. Still, the feeling of solid dirt beneath his own boots bolstered Victor's spirits--until about the third step, when he tripped over a body.

Victor managed not to fall on his face (which he considered an accomplishment) or cry out in dismay (which he considered an even bigger accomplishment). He flailed his arms for balance, then looked up at Lady Fenvale. "Is he...?"

"Only unconscious," Lady Fenvale said. "Now, give me the bag."

Victor nodded and unslung the leather valise Lady Fenvale had packed and foisted on him before she had climbed out the window. She dug through the bag and pulled out a half-empty bottle of wine that had been left in their suite. She dumped a hearty splash down the unconscious guard's chest, then hauled him up into a sitting position against the manor wall and out of the rain. To complete the ruse, Lady Fenvale tucked the wine bottle into the unconscious man's arms. She nodded to herself, proud of her handiwork, then handed the bag of gear back to Victor. "That should buy us some time, at least."

"What if they see the rope?" Victor looked up to the thin line of braided sheets and bedding hanging down from the open window.

"Let's hope they see the drunk, first." Lady Fenvale patted the unconscious man on the cheek, then stood up. "You're sure you can get the gears on your own?"

"I think..." Victor breathed in a bit deeper and tried to mirror Lady Fenvale's calm. "I can, yes. At least, if I take them from the *Stalwart*."

"Good." Lady Fenvale nodded. "I'll go to the stables and saddle some horses. Once you've got the motive gears, find someplace to hide until I come around. With any luck, the rain will cover our tracks. It might even keep anyone from shooting at us if their powder gets wet."

"I thought the whole point was to sneak around so nobody shot at us in the first place?"

"That too. So just keep your head down, and don't let anyone see you. I'll meet you at the workshop. Good luck."

Lady Fenvale stalked off, disappearing into the gardens. Victor steeled himself and set out in the opposite direction. Even with the rain and darkness, he didn't have any trouble finding the looming stone building of the Cataphract workshop. The enormous main doors were closed, but Victor slipped in through one of the side entrances meant for people instead of stories-tall war machines.

Once he was inside, Victor fumbled a candle out of his bag and lit it. He cupped a hand over the flame and slowly made his way through the empty workshop. The crew were nowhere to be seen, having either joined the festivities or retired to their lodgings elsewhere. The steady patter of rain on the tiled rooftop echoed through the workshop, masking the sound of Victor's footsteps.

The *Guilt of Gold* stood tall in her scaffolding, with rolling tables piled with tools and parts pushed up around the Cataphract's ankles. One such table held the bladed head of the *Temper*'s halberd, freshly pulled out of the *Guilt of Gold*'s hip. In the quiet dark, the workshop had the air of a mausoleum-- perhaps one still under construction, given the tools strewn about. As he went past the worktables, Victor picked up the wrenches and pliers he needed and slid them into his bag, taking care to not clink them together too loudly.

This done, he crept across the workshop, heading to the warehouse in the back. The piles of wooden boxes and crates were even more labyrinthine by the feeble light of Victor's candle. Even still, he managed to get to the back of the warehouse without much trouble, to where the *Stalwart* waited. If the workshop was a tomb by night, then the *Stalwart* was a dismembered corpse, complete with a dusty burial shroud. Victor set his candle on top of a crate of steel ingots, then dragged another box over to give himself something to stand on in order to get at the motive gears in the *Stalwart*'s exposed shoulder cavity. The gear assembly sat there, waiting, like a fruit ripe to be picked. Victor breathed in deeply, finding himself surprisingly calm now that his goal was in sight. For the first time since arriving at Maldrinne House, Victor knew exactly what he had to do. He slid a wrench out of his bag and fit it over the first of the bolts holding the gear assembly in place--

The metallic click of a cocked pistol echoed through the warehouse.

"I told you to stay away, Victor." Marissa Chalment stepped into the door to the warehouse, holding a hooded lantern in one hand and a wheel-lock pistol in the other. She kept the intimidatingly wide barrel of her gun trained on Victor as she advanced. "I won't let you sabotage my work."

"I won't!" Victor's voice cracked. He let the wrench fall from his fingers, then winced at the racket it made when it clattered on the floor. "Sabotage anything, that is. I'd never do that to you-- to your work. Can't you see that?"

Marissa's gun didn't waver. "What I see is someone skulking around my workshop, with his thieving hands full of my tools."

"I, er, I wouldn't say thieving. I was going to put them back?" Victor offered. "After I finished."

"Finished what?" The barrel of Marissa's wheel lock didn't waver.

"Working!" Victor's voice twinged with both fear and frustration. "I mean--it's just--if I were really a saboteur, why am I working on the *Stalwart* and not mucking around with the *Guilt of Gold*? I mean, honestly, it would have been much easier to cut some of the control cables or pour sand into the air intake while you've got her in for repairs."

Marissa squinted suspiciously at Victor. "Then why are you here?"

"It's for the *Huntress*," Victor said, relieved to actually tell the truth for once.

"What?"

"Lady Fenvale commissioned me to repair the *Huntress* so the marquis wouldn't get his hands on her. Right now all we're missing is a set of motive gears, and--"

"--you came to steal them."

"Well, yes?" Victor winced again. "If I'd known things would get so ugly, and that there was so much bad blood between Lady Fenvale and Marquis Maldrinne, or that you were working for the marquis, I never would have gotten involved. But then one thing just kept on happening after another and now if I don't get this part, the marquis is going to shoot Lady Fenvale's dog and have the *Huntress* ripped apart for scrap. Just like the *Stalwart*."

Another click rang out as Marissa eased the hammer of her pistol out of firing position. She thrust the weapon into a pocket of her engineer's apron, then crossed the distance between them, stepping onto the same box of metal ingots so she could raise her lantern up and peer at Victor's face.

"You're a terrible liar," Marissa said.

"But I'm not--"

"I know." She set her lantern down and pulled on a pair of heavy work gloves. "Now hand me a wrench."

With two sets of hands, removing the motive gear assembly from the *Stalwart*'s shoulder went much quicker than Victor had anticipated. Once Marissa decided to help, she kept talk to a minimum, only speaking to ask for a wrench or to tell Victor which bolt to pull next. Victor eased the intricate motive gears out of the Cataphract, then slid the whole assembly into his leather bag.

"Thank you, Mar--er, Master-Smith Chalment." Victor wondered if he should bow, then wondered if he could bow properly with the weight of the motive gears pulling him off balance.

"Marissa's fine." She picked up her lantern again and started heading back towards the Cataphract bay. She kept her voice low as she expertly navigated the maze of stored equipment. "Now let's get you out of here before anyone finds us. You're just about the only man I couldn't make excuses about being alone in here with." She looked over her shoulder at Victor and winked.

"I--" Victor hoped the warehouse's darkness didn't show the sudden warmth in his face. "I'm sure you could? Make excuses, that is. You've always been very, er, convincing."

Marissa laughed softly and led on. She stopped at the doorway to the main Cataphract bay, behind the *Guilt of Gold*. "You can find the way out from here, can't you?"

Victor nodded.

"Good. I'll stay here and clean up. Make sure there's no sign you were ever here. Hell, once I alter the logbooks, nobody will even remember the *Stalwart* had a set of motive gears for you to steal in the first place. Just don't get yourself killed before you can get the *Huntress* running again, all right?" Marissa poked Victor in the chest, hard enough to rock him slightly back on his heels.

"I'll try?"

"You'd better. Now go." Marissa pushed Victor through the doorway, none too gently.

He made it three steps into the Cataphract bay before someone shot at him. The brief spark of a flintlock pan lit up the huge, dark room, followed a split second later by a near-blinding muzzle flash. The crack of the pistol echoed through the workshop, terrifyingly loud. The pistol ball streaked past Victor's right ear and ricocheted from the stone wall behind him. Victor yelped in terrified surprise and ducked back around the doorway, into the warehouse. He blundered into Marissa, who grabbed him by the shoulders and pulled him against the wall.

"You're surrounded!" Rochen Dunsall's voice carried through the Cataphract bay, drowning out the faint sound of rain on the roof. "Why don't you make this easier and come out now?"

"So you can gun me down?" Victor tried (and summarily failed) to sound confident.

"Oh, it's you?" Dunsall said, entirely too casually for someone holding a smoking gun. "I only fired first because I thought you were Lady Fenvale! You and I both know how formidable she is. When I saw someone lurking around, I thought the worst. But now that I know that it's just you, Journeyman Brinden, I've got nothing to fear. Which means I promise not to shoot you unless it becomes absolutely necessary. And even then I may just aim for your kneecaps."

"How kind of you," Victor said.

"It will go much better for you if you come out willingly, friend," Dunsall said. "And don't think you can just slip out the back. I've got men posted all around the building. So be reasonable."

Marissa, having remained silent and out of sight during the exchange, drew her heavy pistol and pressed it into Victor's hands. "I have an idea," she whispered.

"I can't fight all of them," Victor muttered back. "I can't fight any of them, even with a--"

"You won't have to." Marissa turned around and leaned her back against Victor's chest. Her strong hands took hold of his, wrapping one of his arms around her waist while the other guided the pistol in his hand to press against the side of her neck. "Hammer's uncocked, but I'll feel better if you keep your finger off the trigger."

"What are you--" Victor's heart beat faster, both from the danger and from Marissa's sudden, warm proximity.

"Just follow my lead," Marissa said.

Then she started screaming.

"No! Please!" she cried, with the volume and melodrama worthy of one of Carondel's plays. She flexed her forge-toned muscles and hauled Victor along with her as she stepped out of the doorway. Her steely grip kept Victor's hands in place, allowing Marissa to hold herself hostage as she dragged him out into the Cataphract bay. Rochen Dunsall stood on the

116

other side of the workshop, accompanied by a handful of his men carrying lanterns, swords, and pistols. Surprised by Marissa and Victor's sudden appearance, they glanced among themselves, unsure of what to do next. Wide-eyed in affected terror, Marissa called out to them. "Rochen! Don't get any closer! He's gone mad!"

"Taking captives, friend? That's ballsy." Dunsall stepped forward, shaking his head. "Perhaps I've underestimated you."

"Back! Back!" Marissa choked out a sob. "He said he'd shoot me if you didn't let him through!"

"Th-that's right!" Victor played along and tightened his grip on the heavy pistol. "Just let me through, or else I'll--I'll--"

"Go ahead." Dunsall shrugged as he pulled another flintlock out of his belt. "Shoot her."

"What?" Victor and Marissa spoke in surprised unison.

"You heard me. Shoot her. It'll make my job easier," Dunsall said.

Marissa stared at Rochen Dunsall, and her grip on Victor's arm eased. "But we--"

"--quite enjoyed ourselves, yes." Dunsall's tone dripped with innuendo. "And while I might be passingly fond of you, I'm more than passingly fond of getting paid. Especially given the fact that I fail to see how a bumbling idiot like him could get the drop on a formidable woman such as you. In fact, it almost suggests that the two of you are in league, which is something my employer is sure to disapprove of. But he'll manage. You're just an engineer, Marissa, and therefore replaceable. Even if you've got a great set of--"

"Son of a bitch!" Marissa yanked the pistol from Victor's hand, cocked the hammer, and snapped a shot off at Dunsall.

He yelped as he ducked behind one of the rolling worktables. "Shoot them both!"

Victor grabbed Marissa around the waist and dove to the ground, just as Dunsall's men fired a ragged volley. Pistol balls spanged from the walls and workbenches, and acrid-smelling gunsmoke filled the air, making it even harder to see in the dark storeroom. The two engineers tumbled over each other, and Victor let out a wordless gasp as Marissa landed on top of him, knocking the breath from his lungs. They lay there for a moment, shocked and panting.

"Did we get 'em?" One of Dunsall's men spoke up.

"Go and see, you idiot." Dunsall's annoyed voice was soon followed by the metallic rattle of a sword clearing its scabbard.

Marissa rolled out of the tangle of limbs and settled into a crouch. "We've got to move."

"Where?" Victor patted himself down and breathed a sigh of relief when his fingers didn't come back bloody.

"Up." Marissa pointed to a ladder a few yards away, leading to the *Guilt of Gold*'s maintenance scaffolding, and scrambled upwards. Victor followed close on her heels, the marquis' men close on his. Just before he could haul himself onto the platform, Victor's boots slipped on the wooden rungs, but Marissa grabbed him beneath the armpits and dragged him upwards with a grunt. She toppled over, and Victor fell on her in a tangle of limbs and leather work aprons. Through coincidence or quick thinking, Marissa kicked the top of the ladder as she fell, and the henchman right behind Victor yelled a surprised obscenity as he fell down onto his peers.

"That won't hold them for long. Follow me." Marissa dashed across the scaffolding, to the next ladder leading upward. Victor climbed up after her, and they had enough time to pull the ladder up after them. Even still, more shouts and curses echoed through the Cataphract bay as Dunsall's men found other places to climb. Another pistol cracked, and then another. Even though Victor knew the range and dim lighting made accuracy impossible, he flinched with each shot. His arms already ached from when he'd climbed down the side of Maldrinne House, seemingly a lifetime ago, but Victor pushed through the pain, knowing he was in for much worse if Dunsall and his lackeys got hold of him.

"Marissa?" Victor panted for breath as they climbed up to the tallest part of the scaffolding, putting them level with the *Guilt of Gold*'s shoulders. "Do you have a plan?"

"Do you?"

"I did." Victor peeked over the edge of the scaffolding, then flinched away when someone down below popped off another pistol shot. "I was supposed to keep a low profile until Lady Fenvale could come with horses. And I couldn't even get that right."

"At least you're still alive?" Marissa said.

"For now." He wiped sweat from his forehead with the back of his sleeve. Below them, Dunsall's men clambered up the scaffolding, growing closer with each passing moment.

"And I intend to stay that way." Marissa rubbed her hands together. "We've got the high ground, at least. Maybe we can find something we can use to fight them off."

Victor nodded and started looking for some tools, parts, or just generally heavy things that he could drop on Dunsall, only to settle his eyes on the open visor of the *Guilt of Gold*, and the waiting helm-seat beneath.

"I think I've found just the thing."

CHAPTER 16

A Cataphract's helm was, by design, compact. Every lever, switch, and pedal had to be within the captain's reach--there were even stories of Cataphracts needing their entire control scheme redone when a new captain was significantly taller or shorter than the last. Victor and Marissa crammed themselves into the helm-seat nonetheless, awkwardly shifting around until they were mutually uncomfortable, with her sitting across his lap, hunched over so she wouldn't bump her head on anything.

If he weren't so busy being terrified, Victor would have been scandalized at the close proximity. Then again, the heavy, unyielding shape of a motive gear assembly jammed into the side of his torso made it impossible to think about anything indecent. Marissa pulled the *Guilt of Gold*'s visor shut just as one of Dunsall's men made it to the top level of the scaffolding. A pistol ball struck the steel visor, and the crack of its ricochet echoed within the cramped confines of the closed helm.

Marissa groped around in the darkness, brushing the side of Victor's face as she reached towards a switch located over his shoulder. "Activation switch should be--got it!" She cranked the switch in question, and the *Guilt of Gold* shuddered as her alchemical furnace flared to life. "Now get her moving!"

"Ah, right." Victor felt around with his feet until he found the pedals installed at the foot of the helm-seat. He pushed down on one, and the *Guilt of Gold* lurched to the side as it raised its right foot and took a single, wobbly step. In that single stride, Victor realized the difference between knowing how a Cataphract worked, and how to work a Cataphract.

Victor tried a different pedal, and the machine dragged its left foot forward in a stumbling step. Between the darkness and the narrow viewing slits of the visor, Victor couldn't see more than a few inches in front of his face. Not that he needed to. There was only one direction for the *Guilt of Gold* to go.

Forward.

Victor fumbled with the foot pedals, and the *Guilt of Gold* shuffled on. Far below, the sound of overturned worktables and screams of dismay sounded with each cumbersome footstep. The marquis' men fled from the

Guilt of Gold, their small arms useless against the towering war machine. The Cataphract wobbled drunkenly with each step, as Victor alternately applied too much or too little pressure to the foot pedals, making the *Guilt of Gold*'s stride uneven.

"Sorry!" Victor said by reflex. "I've never helmed a Cataphract before."

"She's going to be sluggish. We didn't have time to fully repair the hip joint." Marissa gritted her teeth and wrapped both hands around one of the larger control levers. She pushed on it, and the *Guilt of Gold*'s right arm swung upward, slamming into the heavy workshop doors. It was a slow, clumsy blow but a powerful one, with the whole of the *Guilt of Gold*'s massive bulk behind it. Built more to keep out prying eyes and the elements, the iron lock shattered, and the doors swung open into the night beyond.

Victor marched the *Guilt of Gold* forward, but her left shoulder caught the edge of the doorway as she passed through, and the screech of metal on stone reverberated through her helm. Victor pushed both feet down on a pedal to his right, and the Cataphract took a long step in that direction.

On her damaged leg.

The pedal beneath Victor's feet went slack, and the faint snap of a severed control cable echoed from below the panel. The *Guilt of Gold*'s right leg buckled underneath the full weight of the Cataphract, and she slowly, inexorably began to fall. Victor screamed, Marissa swore, and both of them wrestled desperately with the Cataphract's controls. A fresh jolt of agony coursed through Victor's body as he slammed into the inside of the *Guilt of Gold*'s visor. The Cataphract hit the rain-softened ground with a deafening clatter.

And then all went still, save for the faint tapping of rain on the *Guilt of Gold*'s hull.

"At least I won't have to fix that later." Marissa's voice took on a giddy, half-mad laugh. She clung to the helm-seat with one hand, with the other white-knuckled around one of the control levers. Through luck or providence, she had swung the *Guilt of Gold*'s left arm out to catch her fall and prevent her visor from caving in and crushing Marissa and Victor to pulp. "You still alive, Victor?"

"Nnngh," Victor replied. He wasn't sure how he'd be able to talk, with his stomach still somewhere a few stories above.

"That's a start." Marissa let go of the control lever, then stretched down to grab the back of Victor's collar and haul him into a slightly less precarious position. "We'd better get moving before Rochen and his men regroup."

"Right," Victor managed, even as he fought down the urge to throw up. He pushed his glasses back into place on his nose (making sure his face was relatively intact in the process) and then started pawing at the control levers, searching for one in particular. "I think the visor release should be here?"

Victor closed his fingers around the release lever and pulled. The *Guilt of Gold*'s visor swung open, revealing a muddy patch of ground directly in front of them, not even ten feet below. Rain blew into the open helm, and the cold droplets provided a contrasting misery to the warm ache of Victor's many, many bruises. With some effort, the two engineers dropped down into the mud without breaking anything that wasn't already broken. Mud squelched beneath their boots as they ran, only for Victor to pull Marissa to a stop once he heard the sound of hoofbeats.

Lady Fenvale rounded the side of the *Guilt of Gold*, mounted on a tall, mottled gray horse, with another one trailing behind her on a lead. She reined her mount to a halt in front of Victor, then pushed the brim of her hat up so she could stare at the two muddy and bruised engineers. After a moment, her eyes lifted to peer at the felled *Guilt of Gold* behind them.

"I told you to steal the gears, not a whole Cataphract."

As Lady Fenvale spoke, Victor's heart started pounding even faster, until he clapped a hand over the heavy bag still hanging at his hip. He reached inside and felt around, confirming the motive gears hadn't been damaged. Victor's shoulders slumped in relief as his fingers found them still intact and in alignment. He'd need to inspect them more thoroughly later, but by the feel of things, they were still operable. "I've got what we need, don't worry."

"Good. It's past time we left." She tossed the reins of the other horse to Victor, and he hauled himself up into the saddle. Marissa followed suit, settling in behind him without so much as asking.

"I can explain." Victor swallowed as Marissa's arms encircled his waist. In comparison to how they'd squeezed into the *Guilt of Gold*, it was downright chaste, but Lady Fenvale's presence increased the awkwardness by an exponential amount.

"Master Smith Marissa Chalment, at your service, Lady Fenvale." Marissa reached out with one hand to tug the side of her work apron in a mock-curtsy. "I hope you won't mind me accompanying you? My employment with the marquis has reached a sudden and unexpected end."

"She helped me get the motive gears," Victor said.

"And I got shot at for it," Marissa added.

"You can tell me about it later." Lady Fenvale put her heels to her horse. The mare snorted, then took off at a mad gallop. Victor clenched the reins and did the same, albeit with far less panache. In the distance, off towards the stables, someone shouted in surprised dismay. Victor squinted through the rainy darkness and saw the dark forms of riderless horses charging in all directions. Lady Fenvale must have left the stables open when she'd gotten their mounts.

Marissa tightened her grip around his waist, and Victor leaned forward so he wouldn't fall out of the saddle. They galloped around the small hill and past Maldrinne House, still lit up like a chandelier for the guests' revelry. A dozen of those guests had gathered in the rear gardens, clustered beneath umbrellas and parasols, squinting out into the darkness to see what all the noise was about.

They charged past the crowd, tearing great chunks out of the muddy ground with each gallop. By the time they circled around Maldrinne House, someone must have figured out what was going on. Men with lanterns and muskets charged out the front door and set up a sorry excuse for a skirmish line, attempting to block the path to the main road. Marquis Maldrinne himself stood among them, waving a saber wildly over his head.

"What am I paying you idiots for? Stop them!"

The marquis' men hastily shouldered their muskets and fired. Or at least, they tried to. The increasingly heavy rain soaked their powder and threw off the aim of the few muskets that didn't misfire. Victor ducked against the neck of his horse, trying to make himself a smaller target, while Lady Fenvale just laughed. They barreled straight for the marquis' men, who scattered to avoid being trampled. Within moments, they were clear, at which point Lady Fenvale turned around in her saddle and hoisted her free hand up in the drover's salute.

"That's for the play, Cousin!"

They rode hard through the night, stopping only to change horses. Lady Fenvale had made prior arrangements on the trip to Maldrinne Valley, ensuring they had fresh mounts ready at each inn and way-house along the way--though it took some convincing (and no small amount of silver) to acquire a third horse for Marissa. Miles upon miles of Cataphract road went by in a blur. Eventually, as the sun rose and the clouds cleared, Lady Fenvale allowed their pace to slow. She led them off the Cataphract road and into a stretch of pine and oak. About a half-mile into the forest, they stopped at a small, empty shack. With its sagging, bark-shingled roof and visible gaps in the walls, the shack looked more like the skeleton of a building, rather than someplace people would willingly inhabit.

"Nice place," Marissa said, deadpan.

"It's an old loggers' cabin. I heard about it from a passing trader on the way here," Lady Fenvale said. "We should have enough of a lead by now, and even if we don't, we're far enough from the Cataphract road for the marquis to pass us. We can rest here for a few hours." Lady Fenvale swung out of her saddle, while Victor managed a controlled fall out of his. His knees didn't buckle as soon as he hit the ground, at least. "How are you holding up?" Lady Fenvale asked.

"Nnng." Victor had long since forgotten what it felt like to be dry, unbruised, and stationary.

"What he means to say, Lady Fenvale, is that he's been better. As have I." Marissa slipped off the horse and pushed a lock of sweaty hair out of her eyes. "But we're not in Maldrinne Valley anymore, which is certainly a start."

"Here. Drink." Lady Fenvale took a wooden canteen out of her saddlebags and tossed it to Victor, who barely managed not to drop it. He pulled out the cork and gulped down a mouthful of apple brandy strong enough to make his eyes water. He coughed and thumped at his chest as the liquor's warmth slid down into his belly. It was no substitute for dry clothes and a week's worth of sleep, but the liquor at least dulled the ache in his muscles, however temporarily.

Marissa relieved Victor of the canteen and raised it in a playful toast. "Thank you, Lady Fenvale." She took a swig, handling the potent brandy with little more than a slight flush to her cheeks. "And not just for the brandy."

"You've been rather quick to turn your back on Marquis Maldrinne." Lady Fenvale took the reins to all three horses and tied them to a post set in the ground beside the shack.

"Because his men were rather quick to shoot at me," Marissa said.

"I'm sorry," Victor said. "If you hadn't helped me--"

"Don't apologize. I helped you because I wanted to. Besides, it's better that I found out what a bastard Rochen was now, instead of waiting for him to stab me in the back. Possibly literally."

"But you left everything behind. Your tools, your notes--"

"Can be replaced. Most of the money the marquis paid me is already deposited in an account I set up in Kingsforge. You didn't think I left behind a trunk full of gold, do you?"

"I ... hadn't considered that," Victor said.

"So now what will you do?" Lady Fenvale asked.

"She could stay with me--us." Victor's brandy-wet tongue stumbled over the words. He told himself the warmth in his cheeks was from the liquor and tried to salvage the situation. "Master Smith Chalment is an even better alchemical engineer than I am. She'd be of great help in restoring the *Huntress*."

"I honestly haven't thought that far ahead yet," Marissa cut in before Victor could babble any further. She handed the canteen back to Lady Fenvale with a polite smile.

"Then perhaps you should," Lady Fenvale said. She shook mud from herself like a wet dog, then turned her attention to the horses. "You two go inside, see if you can sleep. I'll tend to our mounts and keep watch. We'll head out in a few hours."

"Sounds like a plan." Marissa clasped her hands together behind her back and arched her spine in a stretch. Victor, being polite, certainly did not notice how the gesture made Marissa's leather apron and wet clothing cling to her enticingly solid figure. Marissa winced as something popped, then grumbled a few creative obscenities to herself as she went inside the little hut.

Lady Fenvale looked at Victor and arched a brow.

"What?" Victor said.

"Just putting a few things together, that's all." Lady Fenvale rummaged through the saddlebags. "Not that it wasn't obvious."

"Wasn't obvi--" Victor blinked, then looked back at the doorway Marissa had just ducked through. He cleared his throat, then stepped closer to Lady Fenvale, keeping his voice low so as not to be overheard. "The relationship between Master Smith Chalment and me is strictly professional. In fact, 'relationship' is perhaps too heavy a word. We were acquainted at university, that's all. Studied under the same teachers."

"You think highly of her?" Lady Fenvale's voice had the slightest uptick in tone, making it more a question than a statement.

"Of course I do." Victor nodded. "That she was given the title of master smith alone speaks volumes. She's brilliant, resourceful--"

"Trustworthy?" Lady Fenvale scooped a bucketful of water from the rain barrel sitting next to the shack so the horses would have something to drink.

"She saved my life."

"For which I am grateful." Lady Fenvale held the bucket in place as her horse thrust its muzzle into it and started slurping away. "If you trust Master Smith Chalment, then so shall I, so long as she doesn't give me a reason not to."

"You're not--" Victor spoke slowly, the words, the concepts materializing one by one in his fatigued brain. "You're not jealous, are you?"

Lady Fenvale dropped the bucket. Victor cringed, immediately regretting having asked such a stupid, petty question. He regretted it even more once Lady Fenvale started laughing. Hard.

"Thank you, Victor." Lady Fenvale dabbed tears from the corner of her eye with the cuff of her shirt. "I needed a laugh."

"Oh." Victor said. "I'm sorry I--"

Lady Fenvale held up a gloved hand, silencing him. "Don't apologize. You're exhausted. Giddy. Which means you're going to say

126

stupider things than usual. Which is why you should rest before you make an even bigger ass of yourself."

"That ... is a compelling argument. Thank you, Lady Fenvale." He bowed shallowly, causing a fresh twinge of pain to shoot up his back, and then hobbled into the loggers' shack. There were two cots inside the cramped room; Marissa lay sprawled across one of them, already snoring. Victor considered waking her up to talk about something--anything--but soon thought the better of it. Instead, he eased himself onto the other canvas cot, which creaked precariously beneath him. Victor lay on his back and wrapped his arms around the bag still slung across his chest. The heavy, solid weight of the motive gears anchored Victor, both physically and mentally. So long as the motive gears were intact, he'd never have to go back to Maldrinne House. So long as he didn't go back to Maldrinne House, nobody would try to kill him.

At least for a little while.

Victor woke with the sun in his eyes.

He squinted against the glare streaming in through a gap in the shack's roof and rolled over, only to see the cot on the other side of the shack was empty. Paranoid, Victor slipped a hand into the leather bag still lying on his chest, then let out a relieved sigh when his fingers traced over the metal spokes of the motive gears within. Victor had slept so soundly that it would have been easy for Marissa to abscond with the valuable part without him noticing.

Not that he expected Marissa to do so, but Victor realized that he just had no idea what to expect. The sound of laughter from outside the shack calmed him further, as he recognized both Marissa and Lady Fenvale's voices. He heaved himself out of the cot, eliciting a stern protest from his stiff, road-weary legs, and went outside.

"--which is when my sister said, 'That's all? I thought you were a tailor.'" Marissa laughed to herself at the joke. She stood next to one of the horses, tightening the straps of its saddle.

"How inconvenient." Lady Fenvale smiled in polite (if perhaps feigned) amusement as she checked over the other two horses' tack. As Victor emerged from the shack, she looked his way and nodded

127

approvingly. "You're awake. Good."

"How long did I sleep?" Victor asked, even though he knew the real answer was "not long enough."

Lady Fenvale looked up at the sun, nearly directly overhead. "It's almost noon, by the look of it. We should get moving."

"Hungry? We saved some food for you." Marissa nodded to a nearby tree stump, where a chunk of dark bread and a few slices of dried sausage were laid out on a square of cloth next to the wooden canteen of apple brandy.

Victor's stomach rumbled, and he nodded thanks to Marissa before he dug in. The bread was dry and the sausage was chewy, a far cry from the delicacies he'd eaten at Maldrinne House a mere day before. Still, there was something more honest, more satisfying in the plainer food. Or, Victor mused, it might just be a matter of his hunger making him wax poetic. He washed down his ration with a mouthful of sweet brandy, and the combined effect of the hearty food and strong liquor had him feeling somewhere close to human again.

"I'm glad you woke up on your own." Marissa cinched one last strap on her saddle, then walked over to Victor. "I was afraid I wouldn't get to say goodbye."

Brandy didn't pour down Victor's windpipe, but it was a close thing. "Goodbye?"

"It's best if we split up. You're more than capable of repairing the *Huntress* on your own. I can do more good at Kingsforge. I have friends at the capital. Resources, too. If I get there ahead of Maldrinne's messengers, I can make sure that my version of the story is what people hear first."

"Oh." Victor blinked. "And what is your version of the story?"

Marissa smiled. "The truth. For most of it, at least. The Summer's Steel festival was an unmitigated disaster, Marquis Maldrinne was a wretched host and employer, and Rochen Dunsall was a drunken lout who fell into a jealous rage once he found out I had my eye on someone far cleverer, far kinder, and far handsomer than he."

"Who?" Victor said.

Back by the horses, Lady Fenvale snorted with suppressed laughter.

128

"Who else has Rochen Dunsall tried to kill lately?" Marissa noted. "Thankfully for everyone, you were able to easily best him."

"Me?" Victor blinked. "Nobody will believe I could ever fight somebody like him."

"Not in a sword fight, no. Or a bar fight. Or ... any other direct confrontation. Which is why you proved cleverer than he, using the *Guilt of Gold* to escape when he interrupted our, ah, assignation in the workshop. A bit unorthodox, perhaps, but certainly not out of character for an alchemical engineer. And since Dunsall was too cowardly to challenge you to a proper duel, well, certain drastic actions had to be taken."

"But I wasn't supposed to be in the workshop to begin with. Marquis Maldrinne already thought I was a saboteur."

"Obviously, the marquis only spread that rumor on his lackey Dunsall's behalf, in order to slander your name."

"What about Lady Fenvale?" Victor asked, glancing over Marissa's shoulder to gauge her reaction. "How does she fit into the story?"

"I'm always happy to help rescue a distressed damsel." Lady Fenvale's voice was dry and deadpan.

"That, and it gave her a perfect excuse to leave the Summer's Steel early, so she wouldn't have to subject herself to more of the marquis' entertainments," Marissa added. "Moreover, Lady Fenvale was even so kind as to offer me sanctuary at Fenvale Manor. Which, sadly, I must decline, having caused enough scandal as is. I couldn't bear to be further trouble. Which is why we must part--you to your duties, and I to visit my sister in the capital."

Victor frowned. He could run stress-load calculations in his head without trouble, but Marissa's increasingly convoluted story made his head hurt. "This sounds like something out of one of Carondel's plays."

"Exactly." Marissa patted Victor on the arm. "And, more importantly, it's entertaining. So long as the gossips of Kingsforge hear my story first, that's what they'll believe. It'll make for good gossip even if it's untrue. Especially if it's untrue."

"Furthermore, it obscures the reason we went to my cousin's estate in the first place." Lady Fenvale nodded to the bag of parts still slung across Victor's chest. "So long as they're gossiping about how much of a mess you made, I doubt anyone will think to perform a parts inventory."

"Don't worry," Marissa chimed in again, cheery. "Most everyone will forget about it before long. High society has a short memory, especially when there's more interesting gossip to be had. And the *Huntress* on the march again should be quite interesting."

Victor drank down another gulp of brandy. "That's not as reassuring as you think it is."

Marissa took the canteen from Victor, corked it, and slid it into a pocket of her leather apron. "Believe me, Victor. I know exactly what I'm doing. You just get the *Huntress* up and running."

"I will." Victor patted the bag holding the motive gears. "I've been through too much already to quit now."

"That's the spirit! I'll meet you in Kingsforge. But until then, something to remember me by." Marissa's strong hands grabbed twin handfuls of Victor's doublet and pulled him into a kiss. It was brief, but still enough to leave him reeling. Victor held fingers to his tingling lips and could only watch in shocked silence as Marissa mounted one of the horses, waved her farewell, and set off at a trot. "Goodbye, darling! Goodbye, Lady Fenvale!"

Lady Fenvale tipped her hat to the departing master smith, then went back to fastening the last few buckles and straps on her own horse's saddle. Once she finished, she walked over to Victor and snapped her fingers in front of his still-stunned face.

"Closer to the truth than I thought," Lady Fenvale said.

CHAPTER 17

As they neared Fenvale Manor, Lady Fenvale became more quiet and withdrawn. Victor couldn't blame her for it; Marquis Maldrinne had claimed Count Fenvale was on his deathbed, and there was no way to learn otherwise than to see firsthand. And even if the marquis had lied about such a thing, the count wasn't in the best of health to begin with.

Lady Fenvale spurred her horse, sprinting the last mile to the manor house. Turquo, ever unflappable in his dark waistcoat, met them at the front door. Lily was there too; the dog barked and capered in excitement at the return of her mistress. Lady Fenvale jumped out of her saddle before her horse came to a full stop, handed her reins to Turquo with one hand, and gave Lily a scratch behind the ears with the other.

"How is he?" Lady Fenvale's normally even voice was ragged with fatigue.

"Resting," Turquo said with a solemn nod. "Dr. Polvo informed me that your father should recover shortly so long as he doesn't exert himself. I'm afraid he left yesterday, otherwise he could give you the prognosis himself."

Lady Fenvale's shoulders slumped in relief. "Maldrinne knows you sent for a doctor. He's already planning for Father's death."

Lily leaned against Lady Fenvale and let out a whine.

"In that case, I hope your visit was a productive one," said Turquo.

"Victor has what we need to get the *Huntress* running, yes." She turned around to regard Victor as he stiff-leggedly climbed out of his saddle. "When can you start putting my machine back together?"

"There's nothing to stop me from starting immediately."

"Then do so," Lady Fenvale said curtly. "Turquo will get you whatever you need." Lady Fenvale sagged and leaned lightly on Lily's canine bulk to stay upright. The tension that had kept her moving for the last few days had finally drained away, leaving her exhausted. "I need to see my father." She stumbled a step but caught herself before she fell on her face. Lily whined again and stuck close to Lady Fenvale's side as the two of them went through Fenvale Manor's front doors.

Victor watched her go inside. In the few weeks he'd known her, Lady Fenvale had proved nothing short of invincible. To see her in pain and distress seemed profoundly wrong somehow, as if some fundamental rule of the universe had been suddenly broken, and there was nothing he could do to help.

Nothing, except what he'd been hired to do in the first place.

The *Huntress* was just as he'd left her, half draped in canvas. The armor plating on her right leg lay unbolted and open, revealing the complex mechanisms inside. Victor took the *Stalwart*'s motive gears out of the bag, set them on his workbench, then pored over them with a magnifying lens, making sure they hadn't been damaged or knocked out of alignment during the last few days of mad travel. Once he was confident the parts were intact, he turned his attention to the *Huntress*. Victor wiped out the empty knee cavity with a rag, then bolted the motive gear assembly into place. With the mechanism secure, he started connecting the gears to the rest of the *Huntress*' complex web of control cables and piping.

Victor's aches and fatigue didn't magically disappear as soon as he started to work, but the task was a welcome distraction. It was, after all, something he was good at. As an added bonus, he was already filthy with horse sweat and road dust, so a little extra grease under his fingernails (or smeared over his clothing) didn't matter. As it got darker outside, Victor lit oil lanterns, hung them from rings set in the carriage house's walls, and got back to work. Piece by piece, bolt by bolt, Victor integrated the new motive gears into the *Huntress*' knee until the mechanism was fully connected.

At some point, Turquo brought a bottle of wine and a roast chicken, leaving them on his workbench. The chicken was cold by the time Victor finally thought to eat it, but it was still delicious and far more tender than the trail rations they'd had on the road. Victor nibbled on a drumstick as he surveyed his handiwork. The *Huntress* was ready--for testing, at least. He still needed to calibrate the tension of the control cables. Too loose, and any slack in the cabling would slow the *Huntress*' movement and response speed. Too tight, and the cables might snap under the pressure and cripple the Cataphract. He strung the cables at a safe level of tautness, but he knew he'd have to adjust them later. But before he could, he'd need Lady Fenvale at the helm.

Victor opened the carriage house door and peered out into the night. Fenvale Manor was dark, save for one window up on the third floor: the count's bedchambers, no doubt. He couldn't see any figures silhouetted against the window, nor could he hear anything at that distance, but he knew that's where Lady Fenvale would be. And where she could stay, for the time being. Victor knew nothing he could say or do could help Count Fenvale--or Lady Fenvale, for that matter. Bothering her with something so trivial as a knee adjustment would be blithely ignorant at best. At worst, cruel and callous. And so, Victor stayed in the relative safety of the carriage house. Whatever happened, he figured Turquo would come by when there was news--one way or another. He closed the doors, put out the oil lamps, and prepared for bed.

A fresh twinge of pain throbbed from Victor's knees as he sat down on the cot he'd dragged into the carriage house so many weeks ago. He poured some of the wine into a battered copper mug and took a long drink. Exhaustion set in, and he fell asleep before he could refill his cup.

Victor woke to the crack of a pistol.

Already trembling with surprise, he rolled out of his cot and onto the floor. More shouting and shooting came from the other side of the carriage house door, along with the heavy sound of hoofbeats. He stayed on the floor for a long moment, in case another volley was coming. To his relief, no musket balls buzzed overhead. Carefully, quietly, Victor got back to his feet and crossed the carriage house so he could peek out through a gap in the doors.

Victor squinted against the late-morning sun (how long had he slept?) and focused on the men circling around Fenvale Manor. They surrounded the main house, firing pistols off into the air with enthusiasm, if not accuracy. The muzzle of a long musket poked from one of Fenvale Manor's narrow windows and belched smoke and fire in retaliation. One of the riders swore, dropping his wheel lock to the ground as he grabbed at his wounded arm, while his fellows just laughed and galloped their horses back towards the tree line, out of musket range. As the armed horsemen regrouped and reloaded, they chatted and joked with each other, as if playing some mad game instead of fighting for their lives.

Victor looked back at the main house just in time to see the rear door open. Lady Fenvale, decked out in bandoliers and sword belts, took a step out, but Victor wasn't the only one who spotted her. One of the horsemen let out a cry, and they charged forward once again. Lady Fenvale snapped off a quick shot with one of her flintlocks, and the riders replied in turn with a volley of their own. Lady Fenvale ducked back into the manor house as pistol balls slammed into the stone walls around her. The riders whooped and laughed and set to circling the main house once again. As they passed by the carriage house, Victor got a better look at the well-dressed, well-armed men, and at Rochen Dunsall, riding at their head. The big, bearded man rallied his men with cheerful, obscene shouts, then led them away when someone on the second floor fired another musket. Victor watched the back-and-forth play out a second time, and then a third, each charge and retreat accompanied by shots and ever-thickening clouds of gun smoke.

Tactics and strategy were never part of Victor's studies at university, but math certainly was. And the numbers were not on the Fenvales' side. Even if Lady Fenvale and Lily could account for several men apiece (which Victor had no doubt they could), Dunsall had enough horsemen with him to easily tilt the battle in his favor. In fact, Dunsall had enough horsemen with him that he could storm Fenvale Manor easily, but he didn't. Instead, the raiders kept circling the house, howling like hunting dogs that had treed their quarry. But why the delay? Was it just another cruelty on Dunsall's part, or were they stalling? Waiting for someone to arrive? But who?

The ground shook, and Victor had his answer.

Dunsall's men cheered, and the ground shook again from the unmistakably heavy tread of an approaching Cataphract. Fenvale Manor blocked Victor's view of the main road, but he knew exactly what was coming.

The *Guilt of Gold* marched up to Fenvale Manor--then followed the route Dunsall had taken, circling slowly around the house, as if to make sure that anyone inside got a good look at their approaching doom, no matter where they were in the house. The Cataphract passed by the carriage house, close enough to make Victor's tools rattle on their workbenches. Victor cringed away from his spot at the door, scrambling back before Marquis Maldrinne could kick the door in and crush him like an insect.

The *Guilt of Gold* walked past without slowing down.

Victor stared at the door, at the tall, passing shadow of the *Guilt of Gold*--and pieces started falling into place. Dunsall and his men didn't know about the *Huntress*, or else they would have moved to secure it. Marquis Maldrinne must have sent them to stall the Fenvales, to prevent them from escaping before he could arrive with his slower Cataphract. Victor rubbed at his face, realizing that Dunsall and his men didn't know about him, either. If he were quiet and clever, he might be able to make it to the stables, saddle a horse, and escape.

But then what?

With Lady Fenvale and the others trapped inside the house, they were at the mercy of Marquis Maldrinne. But so long as Victor remained unseen, he had the advantage of surprise, however small. He could help Lady Fenvale. He had to help Lady Fenvale. He was the only one who could.

Victor started to plan.

There were any number of tools scattered around the carriage house that were heavy enough to use as improvised weapons, but Victor dismissed the thought. He had no illusions about his own skill or bravery. If he were lucky, he might get the chance to bash one of Dunsall's men over the head with a wrench, but the rest of them would no doubt shoot him or ride him down or hack him to bits (or all three) moments after he did.

Or was he looking at it the wrong way?

Victor knew he was no soldier; he was an engineer. He didn't fight; he fixed problems. And at that moment, he had a three-story tall problem with black armor and a broadsword to deal with. The *Huntress* was the most logical solution. But while the Cataphract was operational, Victor knew he couldn't captain her. He'd barely been able to stagger the *Guilt of Gold* a few steps before tripping and didn't expect he'd do any better with Lady Fenvale's Cataphract. Marquis Maldrinne could make short work of the *Huntress* with Victor at the helm, provided Victor didn't accidentally crash the white-armored Cataphract into Fenvale Manor first. The *Huntress* would need someone who knew what they were doing at the helm, and the only people qualified to captain her were trapped inside the main house.

Logically, Lady Fenvale was likely thinking the same thing. But with Dunsall's horsemen, and now the marquis' Cataphract blocking the way to the *Huntress*, the Fenvales were cut off from their greatest weapon, a weapon that Marquis Maldrinne didn't even know they had. Victor looked over his tools and equipment again. If he could clear a path from Fenvale Manor to the carriage house, or create some sort of distraction--

Outside, the *Guilt of Gold*'s visor opened with a creak, and soon Marquis Maldrinne's voice carried across the open ground, amplified by a speaking cone held in front of his mouth.

"Hello, Cousin! Hello, Uncle! Have I come at a bad time?"

Dunsall and his men laughed obligingly at their master's jest.

"I apologize for being so late--it took quite some time to clean up the mess you made. Damned inconvenient that your scoundrel ran off with my chief engineer, but the apprentices were able to get things back in working order without much trouble. That's what you get for hiring university dropouts, you know. That idiot of yours couldn't even break things properly. Ha!"

Victor tuned out the marquis' gloating and focused on his work. He couldn't count on Marquis Maldrinne talking forever--each second was precious. The stone walls of Fenvale Manor might be able to stop pistol balls, but the *Guilt of Gold* could reduce the whole house to rubble in a matter of minutes. Would Lady Fenvale be able to keep him talking? Victor lifted two oil lamps from their hooks and set them on a workbench next to the other parts he needed. Luckily, Victor's design was simple to the point of ugliness, and the marquis loved the sound of his own voice.

"But that's just a trivial matter, compared to my birthright." Marquis Maldrinne's sneer was audible even through the hollow echo of his speaking cone. "After your frankly embarrassing abuse of my hospitality, I've decided to collect on it early. It's only a matter of time before the count passes. Provided he hasn't already, of course. I demand that you open the doors and allow me to pay my last respects."

"Piss off, you worthless fop! I'm not dead yet!" Count Fenvale's voice was shrill, ragged, and distinctly alive. A musket fired, and its ball spanged off the *Guilt of Gold*'s steel armor. Victor cringed as the marquis' men returned fire, even though he knew the shots weren't aimed at him.

Soon enough, they would be.

"Obscenity is beneath you, Uncle!" A quaver in the marquis' voice showed him far less confident than a moment before.

Victor lit the two oil lamps he'd modified, adjusting their wicks so flame threatened to escape from the top of the glass chimneys. This done, he pushed a heavy wooden box in front of the carriage house's doors, then set the two oil lamps on top of it. It took one more trip back to the workbench to get the last part he needed; a long, flat leaf spring that had once been part of a fancy carriage's suspension. Victor wedged one end of the spring against the side of the box, jamming it roughly into place until it could stand straight up without his assistance. He ran calculations in his head, verifying the relative insanity of his plan. Then again, it was the only thing he could think of, so it would have to do.

The first oil lamp hung heavy in Victor's hand as he braced a shoulder against the carriage house doors and shoved them open. One of the riders spotted Victor and pointed him out with a shout. "Look! It's the saboteur!"

"He's mine!" Dunsall belted out a wicked laugh, then spurred his horse forward to ride Victor down. Victor stood his ground and hurled his oil lamp into Dunsall's path. Glass shattered on the ground, spreading a patch of burning oil, which lit the grease-soaked rags wrapped around the now-broken glass. The flames stalled Dunsall's charge, and the greasy black smoke blocked his line of sight--for a short while, at least.

Marquis Maldrinne whipped his head towards the source of the commotion. "Hold, Dunsall! I want to make an example of this one! Let my cousin watch as I crush her pet idiot."

The marquis set his speaking cone aside and dropped back into the *Guilt of Gold*'s helm-seat. The Cataphract's visor slammed shut with a clang, and she slowly turned to bear down on Victor. The *Guilt of Gold*'s armored boots left deep footprints in the grass as she closed in. Victor dashed back into the carriage house to his contraption. He put the second oil lamp into a wicker basket he'd hastily lashed onto the other end of the leaf spring, then grabbed the length of metal with both hands and pulled back with all his weight. With the other end braced against a box of scrap metal, the steel flexed into a deep arc. Victor's arms burned as he held the spring in place. He forced himself to hang on, to wait for the right moment: a moment that came when *Guilt of Gold* loomed large in the open doorway.

Victor let go of the spring, jumping back so the end wouldn't tear something out of him as it whipped forward. The improvised catapult bucked, and the oil lamp tumbled end-over-end through the air until it shattered against the *Guilt of Gold*'s breastplate. Thick black smoke rose from the point of impact, but the armor beneath held firm. Victor knew the flaming oil couldn't do more than dirty the tempered steel of the *Guilt of Gold*'s plating, but it didn't have to. A curtain of smoke billowed out in front of the *Guilt of Gold*'s visor, into the visor through its viewing slits, to blind and choke Marquis Maldrinne.

A giddy, half-mad laugh escaped Victor's lips. It had worked! Even as he savored the victory, his mind raced with ideas to improve the design. Varying mixes of different flammable substances might make the smoke thicker, or burn longer, and the delivery method itself could be improved exponentially through the use of a ratcheting winch and a proper release mechanism--

Marquis Maldrinne lashed out blindly, and the *Guilt of Gold*'s broadsword cut through the air. Even on a hasty, misaimed backswing, the enormous blade smashed into the carriage house with enough force to shatter timbers like kindling. A heavy length of oak flew through the air and hammered Victor onto the floor. He wheezed, trying to reclaim the breath that had been suddenly knocked from his lungs, only for a new agony to lance up from his side. A broken rib? A perforated lung? Victor suddenly wished he'd taken more medicine classes at university. He tried to shove the beam off but lacked the strength or leverage to move it. He flopped back onto the ground just as the *Guilt of Gold* hacked again, reducing the old, dry wood to so many splinters. At least the sword fell short of the *Huntress*, tucked as she was at the back of the carriage house, half-hidden beneath canvas.

Too late, Victor recognized the fatal flaw in his plan; he'd blinded the *Guilt of Gold*, but he hadn't disabled her. Victor pushed at the beam holding him down again, to little avail. He coughed, painfully, and hoped that Lady Fenvale would at least seize the distraction--

--and there she was.

Lady Fenvale sprinted through the chaos of the carriage house, dodging past falling lumber and flying splinters. She skidded to a halt next to Victor and dropped her saber, freeing both hands to haul on the heavy chunk of lumber pinning him in place. Veins bulged on her neck as Lady Fenvale put her steely muscle to the task. The beam shifted an inch, then two, and Victor sucked in a desperate, gasping breath and clawed his way out from under the heavy debris. Lady Fenvale dropped the beam and hauled Victor to his feet, half-dragging him deeper into the carriage house even as the *Guilt of Gold* smashed through what was left of the tall doors. They took refuge in the *Huntress*' shadow, hiding from Marquis Maldrinne and his men--however temporarily.

"Did you fix her?" Lady Fenvale yelled into Victor's ear to be heard over the din of breaking wood and clanking Cataphract. "Can she fight?"

"In theory?" Victor seized on the technical details, something he actually knew about. "I mean, I still have some calibration work to do before she's operating at full efficiency. And I haven't replaced the plating over her right knee, either, so she'll be vulnerable there. But she's operable."

Lady Fenvale's lips turned back in a familiar, wolfish smile. "Then it's time to put your work to the test."

CHAPTER 18

Blue smoke chugged from the *Huntress'* exhaust vents.

At the helm, Lady Fenvale pulled levers and opened valves with professional efficiency. Each action brought the Cataphract one step closer to her full capabilities, one step closer to fighting shape. The *Huntress'* joints creaked and clanked--Victor could even see the motive gears within her exposed right knee turn. The *Huntress* clambered to her feet, canvas still hanging around her like an old cloak. As the Cataphract rose, Lady Fenvale leaned out of the open helm to bark out orders. "Find someplace safe, Victor! I'll take it from here!"

Before Victor could note there were very few "safe" places to be found, Lady Fenvale shut the *Huntress'* slotted visor. Fallen timbers snapped beneath her Cataphract's wagon-sized feet as she stomped out of the workshop. Victor followed in her wake, trying to keep close enough that he could put the war machine between himself and any of the marquis' men, but far enough away that he wouldn't be trodden underfoot.

Outside, the *Guilt of Gold* stood with black smoke still wafting through her visor. Marquis Maldrinne might not have been able to see what was happening, but there was no doubt he could hear, could feel the approach of the other Cataphract. The *Guilt of Gold* swung her sword in a clumsy backhand, but the *Huntress* sidestepped the slash and slammed her shoulder into her black-armored opponent, staggering her.

While the Cataphracts grappled, Victor sprinted for Fenvale Manor, clutching at his bruised side. Rochen Dunsall and his men didn't shoot at him; they must have been out of ammunition, or simply distracted by the battling war machines. Victor found the rear door unlocked and burst through. Any relief he might have felt was short-lived, as the first thing he saw once he got through the door was the yawning darkness of a musket's muzzle.

"Don't shoot! It's me!" Victor's voice cracked as he held his hands up in the air.

"My apologies." Turquo lowered the gun. "If you would step away from the door, I'd like to keep the line of fire clear."

"Right." Victor stumbled out of the way.

Turquo stepped past Victor and shut the door. "I've got several more muskets loaded, if you would like one."

"Er, no, thank you."

"The offer is open," Turquo said. The floorboards rattled as one of the Cataphracts outside laid into the other, but the old valet didn't so much as flinch. "If I might make a suggestion, you would have a better view of the goings-on from one of the upper floors. There's a servants' stairway to your left. I shall stay here and hold the ground floor."

"Right. I mean, left. Right. I understand." Victor nodded. He limped to the winding stairwell and climbed upwards, finally emerging out into a long hallway lit by narrow windows. The acrid smell of gunsmoke hung in the air, and spent muskets were propped against the walls, waiting to be reloaded. Victor crouched beside the closest window, which put him roughly at eye level with the Cataphracts outside.

The *Huntress* squared off with the *Guilt of Gold*. They'd broken their grapple, and the *Guilt of Gold* had retreated several Cataphract-length paces to get some distance. The last of Victor's smoke had finally burned off, and Marquis Maldrinne had opened his Cataphract's visor for better ventilation. The marquis' face and clothes were stained with smoke, and his eyes burned with malice.

"So it's come to this, then?" Marquis Maldrinne coughed out a laugh. He twisted a control lever, and the *Guilt of Gold* swung her sword around to point at the center of the *Huntress'* chest. "And here I thought the *Huntress* was scrap! Trotting out the old relic for one last hurrah, dear Uncle? Looking for a tragic, heroic death? How long can you keep pulling those levers until your heart gives out, old man?"

The *Huntress'* visor levered open, revealing Lady Fenvale's snarling face. "As long as it takes, Cousin."

"Diana?" The whites of the marquis' surprised eyes stood out on his soot-smeared face. "What in the hell are you doing?"

"What does it look like?" The *Huntress* shifted into a brawler's stance: knees bent, fists raised, poised to attack.

Marquis Maldrinne wiped soot from his face and shook his head. "Just because you can fence and ride doesn't mean you have what it takes to helm a Cataphract, much less beat me. Surrender now, before you hurt yourself, and I'll find some bachelor nobleman desperate enough to take you. Baronet Reverne has just recovered from the pox, I hear. Only made him blind in one eye. He might even let you keep that damned dog of yours, provided it hasn't eaten anyone recently."

"Sounds like you're scared to fight me."

"This is insane, even for you, Diana," the marquis said. "You've never helmed a Cataphract before, the *Huntress* is a worthless hulk, and you don't even have a weapon."

"By my reckoning, that makes us even." Lady Fenvale closed the *Huntress*' visor.

"You had your chance," Marquis Maldrinne spat, then closed the *Guilt of Gold*'s visor in turn.

Metal clanked as the *Huntress* reached up with one hand and grabbed at the canvas still draped across her shoulders. The dusty tarp slid away, revealing her gleaming white armor (and the less-gleaming replacement parts Victor had bolted on). Instead of discarding the canvas, the *Huntress* hung onto a fistful and let the rest drape down to the ground like a heavy curtain.

The *Guilt of Gold* opened with a quick lunge, driving the point of her broadsword at the *Huntress*' torso. Faster than Victor thought possible, the *Huntress* swung her length of canvas in a wide arc, fabric flapping as it whipped through the air. The *Guilt of Gold*'s sword tore a hole through the tarp, but the rest of the canvas wrapped around the blade and hilt, awkwardly binding them. With the *Guilt of Gold*'s sword trapped, Lady Fenvale moved in and swung the *Huntress*' other fist around, landing a ringing blow on the other machine's breastplate.

The *Guilt of Gold* ripped her sword free of the canvas, nearly bisecting the old cloth. The ground churned as the two Cataphracts shoved at each other, until the *Huntress* backpedaled another step, off-balance. The *Guilt of Gold* closed both hands around her sword for a two-handed swing that hit the *Huntress* in the shoulder. With no small degree of satisfaction, Victor noted the unpainted pauldron he'd installed held up against the blow.

That satisfaction soon turned to anxiety as Victor watched the *Guilt of Gold* hammer away at the *Huntress*. Lady Fenvale endured the assault, dodging attacks where she could, trying to catch strikes on thicker armor plating when she couldn't. Between swings, Lady Fenvale tried to bring her

Cataphract into punching range again, but the Marquis kept moving the *Guilt of Gold* back. He feinted, pulling the blow at the last moment so he could circle the broadsword around to hit the *Huntress* from the opposite angle. Sparks flew as the *Guilt of Gold*'s sword bit into the side of *Huntress*' breastplate. She staggered and dropped to one knee--only for the *Guilt of Gold* to hit her again, this time hard enough to send shards of broken metal flying from the point of impact.

The *Huntress* fell, smashing through the last few standing timbers of the carriage house.

Victor stepped back from his window.

"Steady, lad," Count Fenvale rasped. He stooped over, leaning heavily on a flintlock nearly taller than he was. Lily stood close at the count's side and regarded Victor with a mildly unimpressed expression. The old man hobbled over to the window next to Victor's and looked out on the back of the field with a proud glint in his eye. "She's tougher than you think."

Victor wasn't sure if the count was talking about his daughter or the machine she captained. He suspected the count himself might not even know. Still, he looked back outside, where the *Guilt of Gold* closed in, raising her gleaming broadsword to deliver a killing blow.

A blow that never came.

Wounded, but not crippled, the *Huntress* lunged to the right, massive hand grabbing at something in the wreckage. The *Huntress* hurled a half-ton of debris as easily as a child skipping a stone, and the anvil Victor had used to shape armor and parts flew through the air, along with some other timbers that had fallen over it. The splintered wood glanced off the *Guilt of Gold*'s armor, but the heavy anvil hit like an enormous cannonball, smashing a deep dent in her breastplate. Blue smoke began to seep out of the black Cataphract's joints. Lady Fenvale had hit something vital, Victor realized--but not vital enough, as the *Guilt of Gold* still kept moving.

As the *Guilt of Gold* reeled from the anvil, the *Huntress* shoved herself back to her feet and threw herself back into the fight. The *Huntress* hit the *Guilt of Gold* with a haymaker punch, then twisted at the waist to seize the other Cataphract's sword arm. Metal groaned and buckled as the *Huntress* tightened her grip, and more smoke poured out of her exhaust vents as Lady Fenvale coaxed more power from her alchemical furnace. Thick fingers closed around the *Guilt of Gold*'s thumb, and the *Huntress* wrenched it backwards, concentrating all her weight and power on that one point.

The *Guilt of Gold* pounded the *Huntress* with her free hand, but her armor held.

The *Guilt of Gold*'s thumb joint did not.

Cables snapped as the *Huntress* wrenched her opponent's thumb from its socket. The rest of the *Guilt of Gold*'s fingers went slack as their internal mechanisms broke in turn, and her broadsword tumbled from her now-useless hand. The *Huntress* snatched the sword out of the air, spinning it around to cleave into the *Guilt of Gold*'s leg. The blade bit deep, and the black Cataphract staggered--the *Huntress* followed up with another hit that sheared completely through the knee joint. The *Guilt of Gold* fell backward, but her severed leg still remained upright. Without the deafening clangor of the fighting Cataphracts, a heavy stillness fell over Fenvale Manor, heralding Lady Fenvale's victory.

Just to be thorough, the *Huntress* stepped on her downed opponent's chest, reversed her sword, and stabbed it into the *Guilt of Gold*'s undamaged arm, spearing straight through the elbow joint to pin it to the ground. Lady Fenvale left the sword stuck in the *Guilt of Gold*'s arm, then lowered the *Huntress* into a crouch. Both of the *Huntress*' powerful hands closed around the sides of the *Guilt of Gold*'s visor. Metal groaned as the *Huntress* forced the visor open, snapping latches and tearing hinges. Marquis Maldrinne cowered behind his now-useless controls, trapped. With his Cataphract crippled and her visor broken, Marquis Maldrinne had to know how vulnerable he was; a single blow from the *Huntress*' fist could end him in an instant.

"I'm not going to kill you, Cousin." Lady Fenvale opened the *Huntress*' own visor and leaned over her controls, glaring downward.

Lady Fenvale projected her voice loud enough to carry all the way to the top floor of Fenvale Manor--as well as to where Rochen Dunsall and his horsemen waited just outside of the *Huntress*' reach.

"Don't think I'm not tempted. For years, you've taken every opportunity to snub me, to insult me, over and over and over again. It would be so easy to finish you. Or maybe just give you a scar to remember me by." For emphasis, Lady Fenvale slowly clenched the *Huntress*' fist above the marquis' open visor. "But frankly, killing you would be more trouble than I have time to deal with right now. You're not the only one with plans, Cousin, and the last thing I need is someone accusing me of murder. So I'm going to let you go."

Marquis Maldrinne goggled up at his cousin, then slowly composed himself. "I ... I thank you, Cousin. Once the *Guilt of Gold* is repaired, I--"

"I said I would let you go. Your Cataphract stays."

"W-what? Impossible!"

"You're not in any position to negotiate. Or navigate, either." Lady Fenvale laughed at her joke as she looked over at where the *Guilt of Gold*'s severed leg still stood like an impromptu monument to her victory. "So here's what is going to happen. I shall let you and your men return to your estate, where I'm sure you can find some way to amuse yourselves. To ensure your cooperation, my engineer is going to remove the *Guilt of Gold*'s alchemical furnace--"

"What?" Marquis Maldrinne sputtered.

Lady Fenvale ignored the outburst and continued. "--which I shall hold onto for safekeeping. That way, you won't be able to sneak in with a cohort of engineers and repair her when I'm away."

"Away? Where are you going?"

"The *Huntress* and I have important business to attend to. Business I'd rather have you far, far away from me. Which is why I will keep the *Guilt of Gold*'s alchemical furnace in my possession as a guarantee you won't interfere. Once I'm satisfied, I'll return it to you."

"That's extortion! Blackmail!"

"I wouldn't say so." Lady Fenvale shrugged and leaned back in her helm-seat. "All I want is what's rightfully mine. And for you to stand back and do nothing while I claim it. Which is more than fair, given the alternative."

Marquis Maldrinne inhaled a shaky, nervous breath, then spoke. "Fine," He closed the *Guilt of Gold*'s primary activation valve, shutting off the Cataphract's alchemical furnace. The blue smoke wafting from the *Guilt of Gold*'s exhaust vents and damaged components petered out, and her joints (the undamaged ones, at least) went limp without any power to turn her motive gears. "I ... accept your terms."

"Oh, and one more thing." Lady Fenvale reached out with the

Huntress' right hand and closed her fingers around the hilt of the *Guilt of Gold*'s broadsword. A quick yank pulled the weapon free, and Lady Fenvale proceeded to hold the blade up vertically in front of the *Huntress*' visor before whipping it to the right in a fencer's salute. "I'm keeping this."

Defeated, deflated, Marquis Maldrinne could do no more than mutter curses as he climbed out of his Cataphract. Rochen Dunsall made one of his men dismount, then led the now-riderless horse over to meet him. The marquis barked something unintelligible but unmistakably angry to Dunsall as he climbed onto the horse, and soon the whole troop of them turned about and rode away. From the helm of the *Huntress*, three stories up, Lady Fenvale watched them go, as if expecting the marquis to go back on his word and come charging back with a whole squadron of Cataphracts.

Victor exhaled a breath he didn't know he'd been holding and stepped away from the window. His mind raced, already listing the repairs the *Huntress* would require, even in victory. Repairs that would be made all the more difficult by the fact that his makeshift workshop had been flattened. At least he could salvage certain components from the *Guilt of Gold*. In fact, Victor wagered that Lady Fenvale would be quite happy for him to do so. After all, for every part that Victor removed from the *Guilt of Gold*, it would be that much harder for Marquis Maldrinne to get her running again. Served him right.

Beside Victor, Count Fenvale wheezed. He leaned heavily on the windowsill and dropped his long musket, letting it clatter on the floor next to him. He kept coughing, and Lily whined in confusion. The old man collapsed, and Victor stumbled forward to catch him; Count Fenvale was chillingly light and frail in his arms. Between rasping gasps, a smile formed on the count's blue-tinted lips.

"Told you," Count Fenvale said. "Tougher than she looks."

And then he went quiet.

CHAPTER 19

They buried the count the next day.

The Fenvale family cemetery sat at the bottom of the hill, out of sight of the main dirt road. Instead of a granite tombstone, they marked the count's grave with a table-sized chunk of the *Guilt of Gold*'s armor plating: a placeholder until a proper mortuary sculptor could be found. The funeral was a small affair, only attended by Turquo, Victor, Lady Fenvale, and a handful of farmers from further down the valley. Despite the few in attendance, Lady Fenvale marched the battered *Huntress* to the cemetery to stand vigil over her father's grave, as if giving the Cataphract a chance to mourn her former captain. She kept the *Huntress*' visor closed--ostensibly against the cool summer drizzle, but also to block herself off from view. After half a day, once the local farmers had gone home, Lady Fenvale spurred the *Huntress* into motion once again and returned to the main house. She lowered her Cataphract into a kneeling position by the wreckage of the carriage house, then powered her down.

Lady Fenvale's face was a carefully expressionless mask as she climbed down from the helm-seat. Once she had her boots on the ground, she sighted in on Victor.

"She's in your hands," Lady Fenvale said. "You know what to do."

And then the real work began.

Despite the daunting task in front of him, Victor found the prospect relaxing. Since Lady Fenvale's victory over her cousin, Victor finally had the time to do his job properly, without any number of impending disasters or murderous henchmen to menace him. Luckier still, most of his tools and books had survived the carriage house's destruction, even if it took Victor most of a day to collect and reorganize them. There were more than a few annoying gaps in his collection of tools, such as several missing torsion wrenches and a shattered pressure gauge, but nothing he couldn't work around.

Once he had everything in order, he started with the *Guilt of Gold*. Victor sucked in his belly and squeezed through a gap in the black-armored Cataphract's armpit, then followed an exhaust pipe all the way to where her alchemical furnace sat in the center of her torso. Inert, the alchemical furnace was cool to the touch, a stone sphere held in a tangle of pipes and valves. The furnace's surface was rough and bumpy, contrasting the polished metal that made up the rest of the Cataphract's workings. A brass plaque with the *Guilt of Gold*'s coin-and-dagger sigil was bolted to the alchemical furnace to show who it belonged to.

Carefully, Victor sealed the valves leading into and out of the metal sphere, then disconnected it and eased it out of its cradle. He accumulated no small number of scrapes and bruises as he wriggled out of the *Guilt of Gold*'s torso, but those were a small price to pay for extracting the invaluable, ancient device. The alchemical furnace was the heart of the machine, indisputably the one piece of the *Guilt of Gold* that had never been replaced, passed down through the ages since it had been entrusted to Marquis Maldrinne's ancestors in the days of the first Cataphract Kings.

Victor managed not to drop it.

Barely.

He left the alchemical furnace with Turquo, then turned his attention to the *Huntress*.

Over the course of a week, he clambered over the Cataphract, inspecting her from toes to visor. He tightened bolts, calibrated gears, cleared vents, patched armor; all the routine repairs needed after a hard-fought battle. Whenever he needed parts, he salvaged them from the *Guilt of Gold*, but drew the line at transferring the outer armor plating. He didn't know what the exact procedure was for declaring a Cataphract Oath, but he imagined it might look somewhat suspicious if the *Huntress* showed up with pieces of *Guilt of Gold*'s unmistakable black armor bolted on piecemeal. Instead, he repaired the *Huntress* plating with blank, unpainted steel in hopes he could get the right kind of white paint later. If one were generous, one could describe the ensuing patchwork like trophy scars, proof that the *Huntress* had fought and survived battle. If one weren't generous, the mismatched armor was something akin to one of Carondel's stage actors clad in a nobleman's faded, oversized castoffs.

But beneath the mismatched armor, the *Huntress*' internal mechanisms were in better shape than ever. Victor knew she could still march. Still fight. Still win.

He wished he had the same confidence about her captain.

Since the funeral, Lady Fenvale had shut herself in her chambers on the top floor of Fenvale Manor. Turquo brought food up to her rooms regularly, and regularly returned with empty plates, but Victor wasn't sure if Lady Fenvale or Lily was the one who ate it. He only saw Lady Fenvale once or twice a day as she went out to walk the grounds with Lily following at her side. The two of them would disappear into the surrounding woods for hours at a time, then silently return to the main house before it got dark.

Once, just once, Victor stumbled across Lady Fenvale while she was out. While searching for a wrench that might have gotten flung into the woods when the carriage house was demolished, he found her sitting on the ground, a short distance away from Fenvale Manor, hidden in the thick forest.

Sobbing.

The sound was quiet, nearly alien coming from a woman like Lady Fenvale, but unmistakable nonetheless. Lily sat on her haunches next to her, occasionally turning her broad muzzle to lick the side of Lady Fenvale's face, consoling her the only way the dog knew how. Lady Fenvale wrapped an arm around the mastiff and leaned against her for support. Neither the woman or dog had yet noticed Victor, and he decided to keep it that way. She'd gone off by herself in the woods for a reason, and that reason certainly wasn't so Victor could disturb her solitude and babble out something trite instead of comforting. Victor backtracked, keeping as quiet as he could, using the skills he'd been forced to learn while skulking around Maldrinne Manor.

He made it about a dozen paces before he stumbled--and when he threw a hand out for balance, he instinctively grabbed a low-hanging tree branch and snapped the dead wood. In the sylvan quiet, Victor might as well have fired off a pistol.

Lady Fenvale and her dog certainly reacted like it. In an instant, both of them sprang to their feet and spun around, Lily with her teeth bared, Lady Fenvale with a drawn saber. Even in her mourning, Lady Fenvale kept herself armed, though now a black ribbon dangled from the pommel of her sword.

"It's just me!" Victor held his hands up. Like a dam that had sprung a leak, he kept talking. "And a wrench! I was looking for a wrench. In the woods. Which sounds foolish, I know, but a great deal of my equipment was scattered all over during the battle, and I was just doing one last sweep to make sure I hadn't missed anything, but if I'd known you were here out by yourself I would have just left you alone, which is why I'll just be going now."

Victor forced himself to shut up, then spun around on his heel to leave as fast as politeness allowed.

"Wait," Lady Fenvale said.

By the time Victor turned back around, Lady Fenvale had sheathed her saber, and Lily was no longer snarling. Both of which Victor counted as good signs. Lady Fenvale wiped her eyes with the corner of her sleeve. She made no effort to explain the tears, and Victor made no effort to ask about them. "I'm glad you found me here."

"You are?"

Lady Fenvale walked closer to Victor, and her boots crunched twigs and dead leaves with each stride. "I haven't been following your work as closely as I should." She paused, then eyed Victor suspiciously. "You have been working, haven't you?".

Victor frowned. "I would hope that, after all this time, you would have more confidence in my work ethic."

Lady Fenvale's eyes went wide at the retort, and for a moment Victor thought he'd gone too far, that he'd provoked her wrath, until she shook her head and laughed. "About time you learned how to talk back to me," she said, and took in a deep breath to steady herself.

"I ... I wasn't aware that was something you wanted," Victor said.

"It has its time and place," Lady Fenvale said. "A good leader listens to her advisors. If I surround myself with toadies and lickspittles who are afraid to tell me 'no,' then I'll wind up as spoiled and useless as my cousin. I hired you for your expertise, Victor. Don't be afraid to push back if I'm being unreasonable."

"I, ah ... I'll keep that in mind," Victor said.

"Now, tell me, how is the *Huntress*?"

"Your cousin gave her a beating, but the damage is mostly cosmetic." Rattling off the technical details soothed Victor's nerves. "All the major internal mechanisms are intact, and I've double-checked anything that might have gotten knocked loose. As for her exterior armor, I've patched and replaced what I can. It should hold, even if it's not, er, aesthetically pleasing. I still haven't been able to formulate a white paint to match the enamel of the original armor plating, I'm afraid."

"And what about the *Guilt of Gold*?"

"I removed her alchemical furnace, as directed. Was there anything

150

you'd like me to do with it? Besides keep it out of your cousin's hands, that is."

"Are there any special preparations required for transporting an alchemical furnace?"

"A good question. Typically, alchemical furnaces are transported, well, within Cataphracts. Given how rare and volatile they are, it's usually best to install one as soon as possible, and go from there. Still, moving an alchemical furnace on its own is feasible with the proper preparation. You'd want to keep it in some sort of fire-resistant container, if at all possible." Victor rubbed his chin. "It also might be wise to seal the intake and output valves with wax to keep it from lighting by accident. It'd be a pain to clean out afterward, of course, but--"

"That's my cousin's problem." For the first time in days, Lady Fenvale smiled. "Seal the valves, make a box, then start packing your gear. We-- I have wasted too much time already."

"I wouldn't call the time wasted. Especially given the extenuating circumstances."

"Don't make excuses for me." Lady Fenvale drew herself up straighter and rested her left hand on the hilt of her saber, as if presenting herself for a military parade. Victor imagined the pose was more for her own benefit than his. "So long as we have the *Guilt of Gold*'s furnace, we have the advantage. There's no way my cousin can lay claim to the *Huntress* or the rest of my father's holdings without an operational Cataphract of his own. It'd be too embarrassing, even for him. But while I've been ... here, he's had time to scheme. Which means we need to get to Kingsforge as soon as possible. The *Huntress* can march, correct?"

"Well, yes--"

"Can you have everything else ready to travel by tomorrow?"

"Theoretically, if I--"

"Then do it," Lady Fenvale said. "I promised my father I'd take the Cataphract Oath, and it's damn time I followed through on it." She reached out to squeeze Victor's shoulder. He gritted his teeth into a grimace of a smile as her strong fencer's fingers dug into his sore, bruised skin.

Lady Fenvale looked into the distance. "Tomorrow, we march."

About the Author:

Marc Edmond Best grew up watching giant robot cartoons and movies with lots of sword fights in them, which explains a lot. He currently lives in St. Louis with his family and a dog not as brave but just as spoiled as the one in his novel. He can be reached at MarcEdmondBest (at) Gmail.com